SUGAR CREEK GANG
THE
GHOST DOG

SUGAR CREEK GANG
THE
GHOST DOG

Original title:
Howling Dog in Sugar Creek Swamp

Paul Hutchens

MOODY PRESS • CHICAGO

Printed in the United States of America

Chapter 1

IT WAS ONE of the hottest, laziest summer afternoons I ever saw or felt—especially ever *felt*—when the mystery of the howling dog in the Sugar Creek Swamp began to write itself in my mind. I was dozing in the dappled shade of the beechnut tree near the Black Widow Stump at the time, with Poetry, my almost best friend, sprawled out beside me—the two of us waiting for the rest of the gang to come for one of the most important gang meetings we ever had.

Of course I didn't have any idea *how* important our meeting was going to be nor what exciting and even dangerous experiences we were going to stumble onto that afternoon, or I wouldn't have been so lazy-sleepy.

Up to now, every time I'd dozed off, my chubby, mischievous-minded friend had said or done something to jar me out of my dreamworld into the sizzling hot afternoon that was making me so sleepy in the first place.

As you maybe remember, the beechnut tree we were lying in the shade of, is about thirty feet west of the Black Widow Stump where we have so many of our gang meetings—the stump being the most important stump in the whole Sugar Creek territory because that is where the big, black widow spider had bitten Circus' whiskey-drinking father before he got half-scared to death and gave his stubborn heart to God to be saved from his sins. Circus, as you maybe know, is the curly-haired acrobat of our gang, who has to live with six sisters. He has learned to imitate almost every bird and wild animal there is in the swamp along the creek and the bayou, and he's always surprising or entertaining us with a bird song or a growl or grunt or howl or screech or bark or squall or chirp.

The stump is also about forty feet south of the leaning linden tree which overhangs the incline that leads down to the bubbling spring where we get our favorite drinking water and which is about the coolest place anybody can find anywhere to get away from a long hot summer.

"Please!" I grumbled to Poetry who had just punched me awake for maybe the seventh time. "Why don't you cooperate! You're going to get yourself whammed on the jaw or some place if you get my temper all stirred up!"

"Cooperate!" his ducklike voice came back with. "Why don't *you* cooperate? I'm trying to tell you that Sugar Creek territory is going to be in the news—is *already* in the news. Here, look at this in the *Hoosier Graphic!* A picture of the hollow sycamore tree in our barnyard and our old white mother hog with her six little pigs!"

"I saw it this morning," I mumbled back grumpily,

6

"and it's nothing to brag about. Our old *red* mother hog raises her pig family in a modern hog motel, not in a hundred-year-old sycamore tree in a barnyard with woodpeckers nesting in holes in its dead top. Last week our Red Addie had *seven* pigs, all of them with beautiful red hair like mine!"

Saying that like that to Poetry, I sighed a saucy sigh in his direction, rolled over three or four times to the very edge of the shade, and tried once more to sail away into the lazy, hazy, wonderful world of sleep. Maybe this time my doubtful friend would respect my wishes and let me alone until some of the rest of the gang got there, when I'd *have* to stay awake.

Being farther away from my fat friend, the weather didn't seem so hot. A lively little breeze came to life right then and began to rustle the glossy green leaves of the beech tree. Through my half-closed eyes I could see the leaves trembling and, with my lazy ears, hear them whispering like a huddle of girls in the school-yard where we all go to school in the fall and winter and spring.

Maybe I ought to tell you that sometimes when I am alone in the woods or down along the bayou or just moseying around looking for snails' shells or birds' nests, or sitting on the bank of the creek wait-ing for a sleepy fish to make up its lazy mind to bite the nice, juicy blob of fishing worms on my hook, I hear the rustling of the tree leaves all around over-head—and they *do* sound like they are whispering— and sometimes even like they are clapping their hands

7

like it says in one of Mom's favorite Bible verses, "And all the trees of the field shall clap their hands."

All alone like that, hearing the water rippling in the Sugar Creek, the birds whooping it up in the trees overhead all around, I like to pretend I feel like the Indian boy, Hiawatha, in Henry Wadsworth Longfellow's poem. Then I'm glad to be alive enough to enjoy being alive. It's as easy as eating blueberry pie to imagine the birds are Bill Collins' chickens, and the chipmunks, groundhogs, cottontails, raccoons, possums, and even the polecats are my brothers—Bill Collins being me, Theodore Collins' "first and worst son," which is sometimes Dad's way of describing me. Sometimes when he calls me that, it's a joke, and sometimes it isn't.

Ho-hum! Lying there beside Poetry that sweltering summer afternoon, sailing along like Wynken, Blynken and Nod sailed in the poem in one of our school books, I was just beginning to drift farther and farther "into the sea of dew," when all of a temper-awakening sudden, Poetry let out a hissing sound like a tire losing its air after a blowout and exclaimed loud enough to scare the living daylights out of me, "Hear that?"

Not having heard that or any other that, I groaned a grumpy growl, yawned myself back into Wynken, Blynken and Nod's sailboat and snoozed off again.

"I mean it!" Poetry's voice exploded into my peace and quiet. "I heard a dog howling!" He rolled over several times to where I was, bumping my back with his fat shoulder, then sitting up and shaking me by

8

the shoulders. "Wake up, Theodore Collins' first and worst son! I heard a dog howling!"

"A dog howling or a boy's brains rattling—if he has any?" I came back with.

Up to now it seemed that everything in nature had been cooperating with me, trying to help me get the nap I needed—the buzzing and droning of seven hundred or more honeybees gathering nectar from the thousands of creamy yellow, sweet-smelling flowers of the leaning linden tree; every now and then a lonesome crow croaking a cracked-voiced caw from a tree somewhere in the woods; down in the creek the friendly little riffle laughing gaily along, singing a singsong song, which is one of the most musical sounds a boy ever hears in Sugar Creek country, and the hot sun scattering showers of heat all over everywhere.

Even though all nature was trying to help me, the nature of a fat boy who was my sometimes almost best friend was *not* cooperating. "Do you know what day this is?" he asked, and I didn't and didn't care and didn't answer him.

Then's when Poetry tickled my nose with what felt like the feathered flower of a bluegrass stem, which made me sneeze a sneeze that woke me all the way up. Grumpily I growled at my so-called best friend, "I don't care if it's day or night!" I sighed a sizzling sigh at him and turned my face toward the bayou.

"The calendar," Poetry answered his own question, "says that today is just one month since we buried Alexander the Coppersmith, and that gives us some-

9

thing to do today—go up to the Haunted House Cemetery and help Little Jim put a bouquet of wild flowers on Alexander's grave."

That might have interested me more than it did, but it only irked me a little more at my round-in-the-middle friend for trying too hard to get my attention. I *could* have let my mind do what it had done so many times the past month—unroll a story of one of the most exciting things that had ever happened to anybody in Sugar Creek history, which as you maybe know, *had* happened just thirty days ago when a fierce-fanged wildcat as big as a mountain lion had moved into the neighborhood, and my cousin Wally's copper-haired, city-bred mongrel, named Alexander the Coppersmith, had saved Little Jim's life by attacking the savage-tempered feline while it was flying through the air with the greatest of ease straight for Little Jim's throat.

You have to hand it to that nervous, nonsensical, half-hound, half-Airedale for being brave without knowing it, and living a dog's life better than any dog I ever saw. He proved that day to be one of the biggest dog heroes in the country—and maybe in the whole state—by diving head-and-teeth-first into a fierce, fast, furious fang fight with that madcat wildcat. You can imagine what the battle looked and sounded like if you've ever seen and heard a neighborhood dog who ought to know better and our old black and white house cat in a tooth-and-claw, life-and-death struggle for the survival of the fightingest.

10

There was barking and yelping and hissing and scratching such as I'd never seen nor heard before. I watched and cringed and yelled, "Attaboy!" to Alexander while Little Jim beside me, saved by the battle, clung to my right arm like he was holding onto a tree root on a cliffside to keep from falling over the edge and being killed.

"Sic 'em!" I yelled to Alexander, and he did sic 'em, savager than ever, while Circus and Big Jim, Dragonfly and Wally and even Little Jim kept on rooting for that daring dog doing what was natural to him.

It was not only the maybe fiercest fang fight ever fought, but also one of the shortest. All of a spine-tingling sudden, the battle came to a heart-sickening, bone-breaking end. I saw it and didn't want to believe it but had to because it was happening right before my worried eyes. That copper-colored canine and tawny-furred feline all of a barking, hissing, howling, eye-scratching, fur-flying sudden, started to roll over and over and over like two tangled-up tumbleweeds in a western wind, toward the edge of the ledge they had been fighting on, and *over the edge and down they went—down and down and down and down and DOWN!*

Even while they were still falling, my eyes leaped ahead of them to see where they were going to land, and it was maybe a hundred feet below, where there was an outcropping of jagged rocks. I didn't want to see it, yet I couldn't take my eyes away—even if I had had time to. I did see it—and I also heard it.

* * *

We buried Wally's brave little mongrel not far from where he fell in battle, in a sandy place we found on the bank of the fast-flowing canyon river. Never again would we see Alexander streaking like a flash of burnished copper down the road giving chase to a passing car, never hear him at night with his high-pitched wailing squall as he ran with Circus' dad's hounds in full cry on the trail of a coon down along the bayou. Never again would I get to sit on our side porch under the ivy canopy and stroke his half-sad, half-glad head—when I could get him quiet enough to let me do it. As the last bit of gravelly soil was shoveled onto his grave, I realized that at last he was a quiet dog, and would never again get himself into any trouble for not thinking or planning in advance what he was going to do.

A day or two after the funeral we had a second one for the same dog because we got to worrying "What if there should be a flash flood some day or night, and it would send a wall of water roaring down the canyon, wash Alexander's body out of its grave and carry it a mile or more downstream where it would lie exposed to the weather and might be eaten by buzzards or some carnivorous four-legged animal that sometimes roamed the hills of Sugar Creek territory!

It was a sad day for all of us, especially for Wally, and extra-special for Little Jim whose life Alexander had saved. It was too sad for me to even write about it for you, but we dug up his body and carried it in a gunnysack through the woods to Old Tom the Trapper's canine cemetery behind the haunted house where Old Tom himself had once lived, dug a deep hole in the southwest corner under an elderberry bush and buried him again.

I will never forget the time the gang made a special trip to the cemetery to help Little Jim put up the grave marker his father had made out of a slab of birchwood. His mother who is an artist as well as the best pianist in the whole neighborhood and is our church organist, had stenciled a sleeping dog on it, and lettered what is called an epitaph which Little Jim had decided he wanted on it, and was:

ALEXANDER THE COPPERSMITH
Long may he live in our hearts.

There were tears in my eyes as I stood for a minute looking at the mound of yellow earth under one of the overhanging flower clusters of the elderberry shrub—that one cluster being so heavy and hanging so low it was like a ripe sunflower head, almost hiding the epitaph's last three words, "in our hearts." It seemed like we had lost a member of the gang instead of a dog.

While we were all standing and thinking, I took a quick look around at us. Standing nearest the marker, sort of leaning on his shovel, was Big Jim, our leader, his jaw set, his almost moustache like a shadow under his nose; Dragonfly, the popeyed member of the gang, holding his handkerchief to his nose, maybe to keep from sneezing, because he was maybe allergic to the gunnysack we'd buried the dog in, or to dog hairs or to some weed or wild flower around the place; Poetry whose fat face was very sober for a change, who had the darkest eyebrows and the shaggiest; Circus, our acrobat, with his very curly brown hair shining in the afternoon sun; and last of all, Little Jim, himself—last, except for me, Bill Collins, Theodore Collins' first and *best* son—right that minute anyway.

I wasn't the only one to have tears in my eyes, 'cause right that minute Little Jim gave his head a quick jerk like he nearly always does when there are tears in his eyes and he doesn't want anybody to know it. That quick shake of his high-foreheaded head shakes the tears out without his having to use his handkerchief—not any boy I know wanting anybody, especially any other boy, to see him cry.

We all turned away then, carrying Alexander in our hearts like it said on the epitaph, not a one of us saying anything for quite a while, but *doing* different things to make it seem like we weren't as sad as we all felt. Some of us were picking up rocks and throwing them at anything or nothing, others taking off on a fast run in some direction or other, leaping up and catching hold of tree branches and chinning ourselves or skinning the cat—things like that.

And that was the last of Alexander the Coppersmith, the most wonderful, nonsensical dog hero there ever was—anyway, the most *important* dog that had ever lived and hunted and howled in Sugar Creek territory. The *last,* that is, until a mystery dog began howling in the Sugar Creek Swamp and along the bayou at night—and the howling and bawling and baying and squalling sounded exactly like the sounds Alexander the Coppersmith used to make when he ran pell-mell with a pack of other hounds in full cry on the trail of a coon or fox or other varmint that lived in our neighborhood.

When you and your parents and your common sense tell you there isn't any such thing as a ghost dog, that when an animal dies that is the last of his life on earth or anywhere else, and then all out of nowhere you hear the dog yourself *after* he is dead, you get a creepy feeling moving like cold chills up and down your spine.

Was Alexander alive or not? Before the week would be over we were going to find out, in one of the strangest stories that ever happened to the Sugar Creek gang.

Chapter 2

IN THE LATE AFTERNOON of the day we set up Alexander's epitaph, Little Jim stopped at our house to get his bicycle which he'd parked against the walnut tree near our front gate only a few feet from our mailbox. Just before he swung onto the seat of his neat blue racer to go flying down the road to the Foote house for supper, he got a faraway look in his eyes and asked, "I wonder if there is a heaven for dogs."

It was such a surprising question that for a few minutes I studied his face to see if he really meant it, wishing I could tell him there was, but not knowing for sure *if* there was or wasn't.

When there had been quite a few more silent seconds, and still I hadn't answered, he came out with "Alexander didn't get to live even half as long as a healthy dog usually does. It seems like he ought to have another chance somewhere."

"He *will* live in our minds," I thought of to say, remembering the epitaph on the grave marker under the elderberry bush.

"I don't mean live *that* way," he answered, and sighed a sad sigh, giving his head a short jerk. "I mean

16

I wish he could live somewhere in his *own* mind and *know* he is alive."

For what seemed like maybe three extra-long minutes neither of us said another word, but I had my mind made up to ask my parents about it the first chance I got, both Mom and Dad being Sunday school teachers and studying the Bible a lot. We also had a special book in our home library that explained every verse in the Bible.

When I spoke again, I answered Little Jim with "I wish he could too." Then I turned to the rope swing that hung from the overhanging branch of the walnut tree, plopped myself onto the board seat that was the same size and shape as Alexander's grave marker, and started to swing myself, pumping a little so it would seem like I wasn't as unhappy as I really did feel, while that serious-faced friend of mine kept on standing there, his foot on his bike pedal, ready to take off.

"Do you know what?" I asked him as my swing whizzed past on 's way back. When I had swooshed back and forth several times without him answering anything, I let my feet drag me to a stop. It seemed like that curly-haired littlest member of our gang, whose life had been saved by a dog dying for him, was maybe one of the best and most likable boys in the whole world. It made me proud to have him sometimes tell me his secret thoughts which he never told anybody else in the whole world.

When Little Jim still didn't answer my "Do you

17

know what?" I said to him, "I'd rather have Little Jim Foote alive and in his own mind."

Hearing me say that the very special way I said it, Little Jim gave me a quick kind-of-half-bashful glance, then looked away, swallowed a lump in his throat, and for a few silent seconds stared toward the eastern sky above and beyond the twin hickory nut trees that grew at the entrance to the lane that leads to Bumblebee Hill, like maybe he was still thinking about Alexander and wishing there really *was* a heaven for dogs. Then he cleared his throat, swallowed again and said, still without looking at me, "I guess maybe you're my best friend."

Saying that, that neat little pal of mine swung himself up onto the seat of his bike, gave the right pedal a push, and as fast as a firefly's fleeting flash was off down the graveled road toward the Footes' house.

I stood up in the board seat, pumped myself into a high, fast, forth-and-back swing and began to enjoy it as much as I could, the cool wind in my face, my shirt sleeves flapping in the breeze I was making, and thought how good it was to be alive in my own mind, that I was me, Bill Collins, not anybody else nor a pig or cow or any other kind of animal. Certainly I wouldn't want to be a dead dog buried under an elderberry bush in Old Tom the Trapper's canine cemetery, not knowing anything at all.

Far down the road I could see Little Jim, his legs seeming to pump him faster and faster as he steered past the North Road corner. "There," I said to my-self, "goes a boy who maybe really *is* your best friend."

I gave myself a few more easy pumps, and while I was swinging and thinking, I heard myself whistling the words of a hymn we sometimes sing in the church the gang attends: *What a friend we have in Jesus, all our sins and griefs to bear.*

While I was whistling and swinging, my mind took off on a quick fast journey into the past and it seemed for a minute like I was standing at the foot of a skull-shaped hill outside Jerusalem, looking up at a wooden cross where the Saviour was hanging. There were spikes driven through His hands and feet and a crown of thorns on His bleeding forehead.

As I kept on looking in my mind toward the cross and at the Saviour, I began to wonder what if all of a sudden He would look straight down at me and say, "In three more days I will be alive again and I would like to be your best friend, your very, *very* best!"

I gave my head a quick, sharp jerk, and noticed that one or two tears flew out and fell in a dusty place at the base of the walnut tree where there were a half-dozen little cone-shaped holes in the sand, which are ant lions' insect traps for catching flies or ants or the larvae of some small beetle that might accidentally tumble into them—and the ant lions would have a free supper.

Just then a friendly little breeze came trembling out across our lawn, carrying with it the smell of fry-ing hashed brown potatoes. Through the kitchen window I could see my grayish-brown-haired mother moving around the range, and for some reason it seemed like I didn't need to swing any longer.

I quick helped the old cat die, meaning I stopped the swing from coming to a slow stop by itself, and followed my nose to the back door of our house. I stopped first though at the iron pitcher pump, pumped a pan of clean water, carried it to the stand beside the boardwalk, washed my face and hands, dried them on a towel that hung on a nail on the grape arbor post, dampened my red hair, ran my pocket comb through it enough times to make it look neat in the mirror, then followed my nose the rest of the way to the screen door and inside to see whether supper was going to taste as good as my olfactory nerves had promised me it would be—*olfactory* being the name of the nerves of smell, and every boy in the world has forty of them, twenty on each side, and they are for making food taste better and for making him sneeze when something tickles them. I'm going to be a doctor some day, maybe, and so I'm learning in advance as many things about the human body as I can.

After supper and after all the chores were finished and I had washed my bare feet as clean as a tired boy can wash them and was upstairs getting ready to tumble into the already turned-down bed, I thought I heard a dog barking—a series of short, sharp barks like the kind a dog makes when he has chased a squirrel or a coon up a tree and is bragging on himself as excitedly as he can to let his master know he has done something important and for him to please "COME quick-quick! COME quick-quick! COME-COME quick-quick-quick!"

I was too tired to say very much of a good-night prayer to God and I was glad I knew He would rather have a boy get his needed sleep than to pray a long time when he didn't feel awake enough to do it. Besides, I had been thinking about God quite a few times that day and had said different things to Him at different times like Mom does around the house even when she is ironing or washing or baking a pie or out taking care of the chickens.

As soon as I was between Mom's nice clean-smelling sheets, I sighed a worn-out sigh, and sailed off in a wooden shoe, like Wynken, Blynken and Nod in a certain poem we have in one of our school readers— Wynken and Blynken, as the poem says, being "two little eyes" and "Nod is a little head."

Nearly always when I glide off to sleep like that, the next thing I know it is morning, the sun is shining in our barnyard and garden, and the birds are whooping it up with happiness because they have another day to build nests in, eat worms in and have the time of their lives living their bird lives in. I certainly didn't expect to wake up in the middle of the night— *be* waked up, I mean—by a strange sound, a long-toned, howling squall like a western coyote wailing at the moon.

I sat straight up in bed, my heart pounding because the bawling squall was the same kind of wail I'd heard

21

manv a night when Alexander had been alive and was on a red-hot coon chase with Circus' dad's hounds. Even when they were in full cry, my ears could pick out Alexander the Coppersmith's higher-pitched long-toned squall, like you can hear Circus' mother singing higher and prettier than any of the other voices in the Sugar Creek Church choir.

I felt a cold cringe in my mind and chills up and down my spine. The sound of the squalling bawl was coming in through the north window of our upstairs, which is in the direction of the creek, the bayou and the leaning linden tree.

I kept on sitting tense and even scared a little because it seemed like Alexander the Coppersmith might actually *be* alive—not in his copper-colored *body* away up in the hills in Old Tom the Trapper's canine cemetery, but in his *mind,* racing through the woods and along the bayou and the creek bottoms, living a happy-go-lucky dog's life like he had lived before.

I kept on sitting up in bed and listening and wondering what on earth. When, after a few half-scared minutes there wasn't any other sound of a howling dog, I began to get sleepy. "Look," I scolded myself, "you're just hearing things! There isn't any such thing as a ghost dog!"

I sighed again a few times, plopped down on my pillow and was just sailing off again with Wynken and Blynken and their dopey little Nod, when the sound came again—a moaning quavering wail, and this time it sounded like it was coming from the direction of the tall pignut trees which grow about a hundred feet from the chicken house at the other end of our long garden.

Quick as you can say scat to a cat, I was out of bed and looking under the ivy leaves that cover the upper half of our upstairs south window, expecting to see in the moonlit barnyard or garden the shadow of a four-footed animal, sitting on its haunches, looking up and baying at the moon.

I was wishing for Little Jim's sake that his wish could come true, that Alexander the Coppersmith was dead only in the body he had lived and died in, and was actually alive again in some kind of spirit body he could run and play and bark and bawl and squall in.

To make it easy for me to see out the low window, I was on my knees, with my nose pressed against the screen, and that's when I was startled half out of my wits by the sound coming again, a lonely, sad, quavering wail, "Shay-shay-shay-a-a-a!" It wasn't very loud but was as sharp as a worried mother calling her son to answer her when he has already heard her call twice *without* answering.

The "shay-a-a-a" told me the disappointing truth: I *hadn't* heard a howling dog but one of the half-dozen screech owls that live around our place and in the woods across the road. A second later I knew for sure it was an owl when, from one of our garden fence posts, there was a movement like the top of the post had come alive, and a wing-shaped shadow sailed out across the chicken yard, over Dad's apiary, and disappeared among the orchard trees.

Even though I was disappointed and disgusted at a rusty-red night bird for waking me out of a sound sleep and deceiving me into a scared feeling, I remembered Dad's firm order to me and to some of the rest of the gang NOT to kill the screech owls because, as he put it: "They eat a lot of pests like English sparrows which clutter up our garages and barns and spoil our haymow hay, and they also like cutworms better than a boy likes blueberry pie, which saves the farmers a lot of new corn—as much, maybe, as five hundred dollars' worth in one county alone."

As I plopped back into bed again, I must have been a little mixed up in my mind, 'cause my dream was about somebody's mother baking a cutworm pie that looked like blueberry pie; and when the pie was opened four-and-twenty blackbirds spread their wings and took off, sailing higher and higher into the sky, each bird the size and shape of a wooden shoe with wings.

The next thing I knew it was morning, and there was the smell of frying bacon and pancakes coming up the stairs. I quick rolled over and out of bed, shoved myself into my clothes and, not being quite awake, sort of staggered past the big Webster's unabridged dictionary on its stand at the head of the bannister, and followed my olfactory nerves down to the kitchen.

That was one thing I always liked to do—be on time

for breakfast—partly because if I missed it I'd get too hungry before dinner, which I had done only twice in my half-long life, and partly because in our tool shed there is a beech switch lying across the gun rack, and the switch looks better there than it does in a boy's father's right hand. It also *feels* better.

We were right in the middle of breakfast when Mom surprised Dad and me by saying, "There's something special our family is going to do this summer. I just got the idea yesterday from a magazine article I read. It sounded so good I decided it was something our family was going to do."

"*You* decided what *our* family was going to do?" Dad said from under his reddish-brown moustache, which he had just wiped with a napkin after finishing his first cup of coffee, and I was looking at him over the top of my mug of milk I had just reached the bottom of.

"Certainly," Mom answered. "Don't you know that I always make up our minds?" There was a mischievous tone in her voice and a twinkle in her eye. Before Dad or his son could laugh at a joke we had laughed at quite a few times before, Mom explained what she had made up her mind we were going to do: "The magazine article said that life was so full of worries and troubles that we all need a change now and then. The family in the story called it 'taking a happiness break' just like office workers and others take a coffee break. Every day each person in the family gets to do one thing he especially wants to do to make himself happy."

Dad came out then with an idea that wasn't in the magazine when he said, "Wouldn't it make a person happier if he did something to make someone *else* happy? I just read the other day in a poem by Byron that 'he who joy would win must share it, for happiness was born a twin.'"

For a minute it looked like Mom was going to lose the happiness that had been in her eyes. Then she took a sip of her second cup of coffee, set the cup in its saucer and said, "Why didn't the article mention that? I think I'll write the editor and tell him. Maybe somebody'll read the letter and decide to help somebody else to be happy."

For a few jiffies my parents sort of forgot about their son and talked back and forth about happiness, Dad winding up with " 'Give and it shall be given unto you, good measure, pressed down and running over.' We all know who said that, don't we?"

I watched for a chance to get in one of yesterday's leftover questions which was: "Does anybody know whether there is a heaven for dogs?"

Two coffee cups went down in their saucers at the same time, and two voices, one from the end of the table and the other at the side next to the range, asked, "Whatever makes you ask a question like that?"

"Little Jim," I said. "He doesn't want Alexander to be dead in his mind—only in his copper-colored body in Old Tom the Trapper's cemetery."

That question upset Mom's happiness-break plans, 'cause all of a sudden it seemed like she would be happier if the breakfast dishes were washed, and Dad would be happier if the outdoor chores were finished.

Before ten more minutes had passed, we had come up with a plan to let each one of us have his own happiness break at least once a day—do anything he wanted to if it didn't break any family rules or make anybody else in the family unhappy. Also Dad decided he would look in the Bible for an answer to Little Jim's question, the Bible being the only book in the world that has all the right answers about life and death and afterward.

"My happiness break this summer," Mom announced from the dishpan where her hands were getting their three-times-a-day beauty treatment with her favorite detergent, "is to set those three old hens we've got out there in the break-up pen."

I looked out the screen door to the break-up pen by the garden gate where three of our best laying hens were in our chicken jail, which was where we always put any of our laying hens when they stopped laying and went cluck-cluck-clucking around the barnyard all day, cranky-fussy because they wanted to sit on a nest of eggs for three weeks and raise a family of little chickens. One week in the pen and they would always be cured, and go back to laying again.

"Hey!" I said to Mom. "What's Old Bent Comb doing in there?"—Bent Comb being my favorite mother hen, 'cause when she had been a little chicken I had

saved her life after she had been stepped on by a horse
—her foot had been stepped on, I mean—and instead
of letting Dad kill her 'cause he thought she would die
anyway, I had begged him to let me nurse her back to
health. She did get well, though she always walked
and ran with a limp.

Looking out at the three hens in the chicken jail, I
saw Old Bent Comb limping around from one end
of the pen to the other, her feathers ruffled like her
other two hen friends and cluck-cluck-clucking like
the only way in the world she could ever be happy
would be to go cluck-clucking around the place with a
family of cheeping little chickens running all over
everywhere after her.

"My happiness break," Dad announced, "is to patch
the roof on Old Addie's hog house. We don't want
her seven little pigs to get wet."

I almost dropped the plate I was wiping as I looked
at Dad who was at the iron pitcher pump at the end
of the boardwalk at the time, pumping a pail of water
to carry out to the hog trough. "She got her family
already?" I asked, astonished.

"Already," Dad said. "I was going to tell you at
the breakfast table but got sidetracked with happiness."

And so our day was started—a day that might be one
of the most important days in the history of happiness.

Chapter 3

IT TURNED OUT that my happiness was born a *triplet* that day because I not only got to help make Dad happy by helping him patch the roof of Old Red Addie's apartment house, but made Addie and her seven little pigs happy by making sure the next rain didn't turn their home into a shower bath.

"Don't I get any happiness break for myself?" I asked Dad when the last shingle had been put in place on Addie's roof.

"How would you like to dig the dandelions out of the lawn and the sourdock out of the south pasture?"

"You call *that* happiness?" I asked, and gave a sharp wham with my hammer against the end of the hog-house ridgepole.

Dad's answer was in an indifferent voice when he answered, "Oh, I just thought maybe while you were digging them, you could earn one cent apiece for the dandelions and two cents for each sourdock, and in that way earn enough to pay for the new nylon fishing line you've been wanting. Also, there might be quite a few fishing worms under the roots," which is why half of the third part of my happiness break that day was work instead of play. I spent almost two

29

good hours digging dandelions and sourdock, and it also took that long to get enough worms to fill a bait can, when I *could* have gotten enough in maybe seven minutes digging in a special place behind our barn.

Ho and hum and ho-ho-hum! It was while I was in the south pasture after finding and digging thirty-seven dandelions out of our lawn, that I came up with the idea that maybe I could dig all the *other* bad weeds there were around the place for two, or maybe three, cents apiece, and get a new fishing rod as well. To show Dad what a good little weed digger I was, I not only looked for and found and dug out all the dandelions and sourdock I could find, but I found and dug also as many other bad weeds as I ran across—in the pasture and along the fencerow—curley dock, corn cockle, foxtail, Canada thistle, horse nettle, pigweed, and outside the fence of Addie's pen, quite a few jimsonweeds. The jimsonweed is one of the worst poisonous weeds in the whole territory and has rank smelling leaves and violet trumpet-shaped flowers which wind up their year's growth with roundish, prickly fruit. I couldn't carry all the big weeds in the gunnysack I was dragging, but I did dig them out and carry them to the place in our barnyard where Dad could let them dry so we could burn them.

I wound up the morning's hard work with sixty-five fishing worms, seventy-four cents' worth of dandelions, forty cents' worth of sourdock, but got nothing at all for the jimsonweeds I dug, nor for the pigweed, foxtail or Canada thistle.

"You're a very good weed digger," Dad said. "I didn't know you had it in you. But I didn't intend to teach you to become a little gold digger too." Then he gave me a friendly look, took his billfold out of his pocket and handed me two one-dollar bills.

"But I thought you said I didn't get paid for anything but dandelions and sourdock."

"That's right," Dad answered with a grin and with a twinkle in his eyes under his shaggy brows. "The extra is a *tip*. Now let's go in for dinner and after that, no dishes—just take off to your happiness break with the gang."

"Yes, sir," I answered, and started to start toward the washpan at the grape arbor, but got stopped by Dad saying, "One more thing, son."

Dad gave me a level look, putting both hands on my shoulders, and said, "You are going to make a success in life. You'll always be in demand as a worker, and people will always respect you."

Coming as a surprise after I'd tried to gold-dig him, I wondered what else he was going to say, but felt fine when he added, his hands still on my shoulders, and his eyes boring into mine: "You always do your work carefully. You do it well, and you do more than is asked of you."

"I do?" I asked.

"You're not perfect, but you *are* improving, son. And Mother and I are proud of you. You're getting to be so polite, and you are growing like a weed."

"What kind of a weed?" I asked, and then, feeling

like a million dollars instead of only two dollars, I whirled around and took off toward the kitchen to see if there was anything Mom needed me to do to help her get the table set for dinner, something I could do for her free. As I ran, it seemed like maybe the Collins family was one of the best families in the world to have been born in.

One day about a week later, Dad gave me another compliment about what a good boy I was. He and I were standing out by the grape arbor at the time, looking at and counting the royal-blue, trumpet-shaped flowers of the seven morning glory vines that had climbed the seven-foot-long strings that reached from the ground all the way up to the gutter of the tool shed eaves. It seemed like every morning there were more flowers than the day before. Seventy-seven had been the largest number up to now, but yesterday had been a very hot day and it had rained a quiet rain during the night, so today, being sunshiny, the whole side of the tool shed was aflame with what looked like blue fire.

". . . ninety-eight, ninety-nine, one hundred, one hundred one . . .," Dad was counting out loud, while I was waiting till he got through to tell me how many I had already counted, which was one hundred thirteen.

Dad stopped at one hundred seven which was pretty good counting for a father. Then he turned to me and, like he had been doing quite a few times lately, took me by the shoulders with his calloused hands and, looking me in the eyes, said, "First-and-worst son, can you take a compliment before breakfast?"

"If it's not too long," I came back with, smelling sausages and pancakes coming from the kitchen door.

"I just wanted to say," Dad began, then cleared his throat sort of like what he was going to say needed a *very* clear voice to come out through. "You've been doing a fine job helping your mother and me bring up your sister, and we want you to know we appreciate it. You're helping her grow up like a morning glory instead of like a wild grapevine—which reminds me, your mother could stand a few more words of appreciation herself for all the work she does and the way she stands up under so much pressure. It's not easy to do all the housework, keep her men in clean clothes, cook the meals, look after the chickens, and—well, just everything a mother has to do—so it's up to us to help make life easier and more interesting. Maybe a little more than we have in the past."

"Yes, sir," I said back to Dad, getting a suspicious idea at all these words and not being able to think of anything especially helpful I had been doing around the place.

"You and Mom planning to go to town or somewhere together today for a happiness break and want me to baby-sit with the rest of the family while you're gone?"

"Bright boy," Dad said back, then added, "It's that my sister is coming from Memory City today and she thinks you're an especially courteous and thought-ful boy, and—"

"Is Wally coming with her?" I asked, wondering what I would do with my first and worst cousin who, as you know, was Alexander the Coppersmith's owner, and even though I felt very sorry for him that his dog had had to die in the battle with the wildcat, he had always been kind of hard to get along with.

"It's a secret visit," Dad explained. "Wally and his father are going to the fair, and your red aunt, as you call her, is driving here to talk to us about a very special behavior problem she's been having with Wally since Alexander died. She thinks—as I said—that her boy ought to be as fine and well-behaved as her big brother's first and best son, see?"

Mom rang the small handbell she kept on the corner of the kitchen worktable to call us to breakfast and dinner and supper and at any other time she wanted or needed us for anything, so I twisted out of Dad's grasp and started toward the boardwalk that led to the kitchen, saying over my shoulder at him, "You can count on me—if you can count. There were one hundred thirteen morning glories, not just one hundred seven."

Mom had had the phone call from my red aunt early in the morning, so the breakfast dishes were done, the beds made and the house cleaned. We all flew around like chickens with their heads off, dusting and straightening, and also keeping our eyes peeled for the front gate to see if somebody's car had stopped.

After maybe forty minutes of doing what Mom calls "waiting in state," my red aunt came, and she and Mom and Dad had a long talk in the living room while I baby-sat—and baby-*ran*, and baby-*fussed* with my sister, Charlotte Ann.

Once when I went into the kitchen to get a cookie for Charlotte Ann to help keep her quiet and had just helped myself to *two* cookies so she wouldn't have to eat hers all by herself, I overheard through the partly open living room door, my red aunt's worried voice saying, "I wish I knew the Bible as well as my big brother Theodore does. I see the need for it more and more when I am here. I like the way you bring up your children. I'm really afraid Walford is going to grow up to be a little civilized heathen, if you know what I mean—unless Howard and I can get him started going to Sunday school and church. Wally's been so bitter ever since Alexander died. He just can't understand why."

For what seemed like several minutes nobody in the other room said a word, and I didn't know I was going to push the door open and walk in and say what I said. I was right in the middle of saying it before I saw Mom's eyebrows drop to let me know I had been eavesdropping and had come in to interrupt a private talk. This is what my red aunt heard me say: "He died to save Little Jim's life—just like the Saviour—" and then I choked up and couldn't even finish the sentence I had started, but if I *had* finished I'd have

35

wound up with: ". . . just like the Saviour died on the cross two thousand years ago for *everybody*."

My red aunt looked at me and there were tears in her eyes. She smiled in my direction, "Thank you, Bill. Thank you so very much. That helps a great deal."

"It's about time for me to go gather the eggs," I thought of to say, then remembered it was still only ten o'clock in the morning, but left the living room anyway and went outdoors to take Charlotte Ann her cookie.

After dinner my red aunt had to hurry back to Memory City to get home before her men came back from the fair. We all were at the front gate to tell her good-bye and I was standing beside Theodore Collins, my first and worst father, when she said to him, "Our psychiatrist thinks if we could get him another pet as nearly like Alexander as possible it might help, but where in the world could one ever find a dog like that one?"

My mind agreed with that, all right. There never was and never would be another like him—never and never and *never*, as you maybe know if you've read the stories *10,000 Minutes at Sugar Creek* and *We Killed a Wildcat at Sugar Creek*.

Dad answered his only sister by saying, "Couldn't you just stop at the animal shelter on the way home and get some fluffy, cuddly little dog and take him home with you?"

"It wouldn't work," my red aunt said from behind

the steering wheel of her car where she was at the time, ready to take off through the front gate. "He wants a homely, ridiculous dog like Alexander, not some dainty little lapdog type." She glanced down at a dainty little wristwatch on her arm, and said in a serious voice, "You pray for me, will you? I think maybe I'm getting too much on my mind—what with all the troubles in the world, and getting worse with every newspaper. Sometimes I get to wondering if maybe God has sort of left us all to get along the best we can and doesn't care anymore what happens to us."

For a few minutes nobody said another word, while I looked up at Dad's serious face to see if I could read what he was going to answer her. I was surprised at what he did say, which was "Troubles can be good for us sometimes, depending on how we use them. I read the other day where a man was in a far country, out of work, hungry and terribly homesick. He let his troubles start him on a fast run toward home. Long before he got there, his father saw him and ran and fell on his neck and kissed him and gave him a royal welcome."

Dad's sister swallowed a lump in her throat, stared ahead across the road, her almost lily-white hands gripping the steering wheel like she was holding onto it to keep from falling. Then she said to my parents, "There are prodigal *daughters* too. This one is going to start for home herself as soon as she finds out how."

What happened right then was one of the most wonderful things that could ever happen to anybody.

37

My father's only sister decided she wanted to become a Christian *right now*. As soon as Dad had opened and read a special verse from the New Testament he always carried, we had an outdoor prayer meeting, with my aunt sitting in the car and Mom and Dad and Charlotte Ann and I standing outside. It was while Dad was in the middle of his prayer that Charlotte Ann interrupted him by pounding on his knees and whining, saying, "I want to be up where the heads are!"

Mom quickly stooped, lifted my heavy sister, and as soon as I could I got my own red head where my heart already was, in a little corner of the prayer circle, while Dad finished his prayer, part of which was ". . . and be with Wally; help him to learn how a boy can be happy without having everything. Help Lillian to believe that You *do* care what happens to us, that You would rather have us love You than anything else. Give her a safe journey back to Memory City."

When Dad finished, Wally's mother started to pray, her prayer being extra-short because it was interrupted by tears getting into her throat, but I never will forget part of it, which was: "Thank You, heavenly Father, for bringing me back to Yourself again. It's been so lonely out in the far country." That's when the tears stopped her.

A little later her car took off and disappeared in a cloud of dust as it swooshed up the road past the hickory nut trees to Memory City. I stood beside the mailbox looking until the cloud had drifted all the way to Bumblebee Hill, which is halfway to the bayou which, I remembered, was where Dragonfly's mother had thought she had seen a flying saucer and also heard a dog howling.

"I like your sister better every time I see her," Mom right then said to Dad. "I think I married into a very nice family."

"Including even her red-moustached brother?" Dad asked Mom.

"Even," Mom said and slipped her arm through his as they started to walk slowly toward the house.

Right then, I felt Charlotte Ann's small hand tugging at mine. Looking down into her shining eyes, I quick said, "Even," and she and I walked side by side following Mom and Dad. "We were born into a pretty nice family—both of us," I said down to her just as Mixy came running from the grape arbor to let us know she belonged too.

At supper that night, Mom came across the table with: "Mrs. Gilbert called this afternoon. She's *sure* she saw something last night hovering above the island below the Thompsons' place. That woman's really worried!"

"Worry," Dad said, "is contagious like the measles. Let one person begin to worry on a party line, and the first thing you know every husband in the neighborhood has a worried wife to worry about."

I didn't sleep too well that night because worry is contagious, and once or twice I woke up and actually looked out the south window where a screech owl had fooled me the night before, and for a few jiffies I strained my eyes to see if I could make them see a flying saucer landing in the barnyard. If I could I would have something exciting to tell people, the same as Dragonfly's mother had.

But there wasn't even a whisper in the wind, and the Milky Way that was like a pale, star-sprinkled road stretching across the sky, didn't have even one lazy white cloud to shadow it.

I went to sleep thinking about my cousin Wally, and wishing something could happen to make him happy again. After all, he couldn't help it that he had been born with a different father and mother and was a city boy instead of a country boy, and had had only one pet to play with—and never could get the wonderful feeling a boy gets when there is wildlife all around which he can call his brothers, and he has so much work to do he doesn't have time to get lonesome. I had almost *too* much work, sometimes.

Maybe my red aunt was right; maybe if they would start taking their son to church, it would give him respect for God, and he might not feel mad at Him for letting his dog get killed in battle.

As soon as I had satisfied myself that no flying saucer was going to land in the barnyard or in the south pasture, and was too sleepy to care anyway, I crawled back into bed, pulled one thin sheet over me and set sail for the land of Nod.

The next day and the next and next, and twenty or more days went past, taking our short summer with them, and nothing very important happened, except that once a week there was a letter from Wally's mother telling us that her son was still having problems and still wouldn't even look at any other dog, no matter how many different kinds they tried to get for him.

One thing kept bothering me, though—and that was that the newspapers kept on telling about different people in different parts of our nation seeing flying things at night, and right in our own neighborhood Dragonfly's mother kept on seeing things nobody else saw and her own first and worse son was getting more and more mixed up in his mind about them.

One whole month passed since we'd been up to Alexander's grave and it was time to go again, as I've already told you, in the first chapter of this story. It was a very hot day, as I've already told you also. And nearly always on a hot day when I've had to eat a big dinner to keep from starving and to help me keep on growing like my father says—like some kind of weed—I am especially sleepy right *after* dinner, which is why I was so dopey-sleepy under the beechnut tree that afternoon when the mystery of the howling dog in the Sugar Creek Swamp really came to life in our minds and also in honest-to-goodness *life*.

The first thing Poetry said to me when I got there was, "Where'd you get that citified short-sleeved shirt? Boy, do you look cool!"

I gave his round-in-the-middle body and well-worn blue jeans a lazy once-over and in spite of being sleepy managed to think to say, "You don't look so

41

hot yourself." But maybe my just-made-up joke wasn't funny, 'cause there was no one there to laugh at it except Poetry and he didn't seem to think it was very funny.

I was stretched out on the ground, as you already know, when there came floating in from some direction or other a long-toned, high-pitched trembling cry like a lonely loon calling across a northwoods lake. It also sounded like Alexander the Coppersmith when he was running with the hounds in full cry on a red-hot coon or fox trail.

"Circus," I mumbled, knowing there never had been any loons in Sugar Creek territory, and remembering that Circus our acrobat could mimic most any bird or animal he'd ever heard. A half dozen jiffies later I heard Circus' loon call again, this time from maybe forty feet behind us where there is a little thicket of elm saplings. I rolled over, opened my sluggish eyes, focused them in his direction, and there he was, swaying back and forth in the top of one of the elms, getting ready to do what I'd seen him do many a time—reach out and up to the very top branch of the baby elm, swing his body out and ride the green-leafed bronco down to the ground, which right that minute he did, landing with an easy plop, and letting the little sapling swing back up again as fast as a boy straightens up from digging bad weeds in the garden when his mother rings her handbell that dinner is ready.

Something else happened right then that knocked

most of the sleep out of me. Again I heard that lonely, long-toned, wailing squall, and it *hadn't* come from Circus Brown but from somewhere above or around us and from two different directions at the same time. Also, it did *not* sound like a red-throated loon on a northwoods lake giving a twilight mating call, but *did* sound like Alexander the Coppersmith on a coon or fox trail—and it had come, *not at night, but in the middle of a hot summer afternoon!*

"What on earth!" I thought, and was wide awake, very, *very* wide awake.

Chapter 4

THREE BOYS in the shade of the beechnut tree, thirty feet from the Black Widow Stump, forty feet from the leaning linden tree, stared at each other in their startled faces and listened as hard as they could in every out direction there is, as well as all around up.

Had we actually heard a dog howling, or had we only thought we had? And if we had, was the dog a ghost dog or a real one?

For maybe forty-nine seconds which seemed like that many minutes while we listened, all we heard was the droning of maybe seven hundred honeybees working the creamy yellow, very fragrant flowers of the leaning linden tree, the musical gurgling of the lively water in the spring, and the cracked-voiced cawing of the croaking crow.

A jiffy later, nature let loose with two of her other voices: a turtledove's very sad "coo-o, coo-o," and the harsh, grating "kow-kow-kow kuk-kuk" of a rain crow which nearly always sings before or after a rain or when the weather is damp.

"Maybe *that's* what we heard," Poetry said in a disgruntled voice, "not a howling dog. We all know it couldn't have been Alexander the Coppersmith, 'cause dead dogs are deaf and dumb and there isn't any such thing as a ghost dog, anyway."

So that was that, and a very disappointing that, at that. We'd heard a mourning dove and a black-billed rain crow in one of nature's duets and only *thought* we had heard a howling dog.

We settled down to waiting for the rest of the gang. A few jiffies later we again heard the lonely "coo-o, coo-o," and the harsh, grating "kow-kow-kow kuk-kuk" from the trees that bordered the bayou. It sounded for all the world like the lonely wail of a lost ghost dog—only this time the cracked voice of the croaking crow joined in to make it a trio instead of a duet: a mourning dove soprano, a rain crow alto and the rasping, high-pitched tenor of the cawing crow.

Ho-hum! Maybe it was because we all wanted something exciting to do or to worry about that it was a pretty big letdown, like blowing up a monster soap bubble, only to have it all of a sudden burst and spatter your face with what is left of it.

Poetry went back to doing what he had been doing in the first chapter of this story, turning the pages of the *Hoosier Graphic* and reading different things. I went back to what *I* had been doing, which was trying to catch up on wanted sleep, and Circus, after turning a couple of cartwheels, dropped down panting beside me.

"You guys want to hear the society news?" Poetry's squawking ducklike voice asked. Without waiting for us to say yes or no, he began to read from what is called the society column, which is always Mom's first place in the paper to read: "Seneth Paddler left Friday for his annual vacation in California. . . . Several local residents have revived the flying saucer mystery by reporting seeing strange colored lights in the swamp below the Paddler cabin. A saucer-shaped object above the Sugar Creek Cave was seen moving silently in widening circles, then hovering for a full three minutes before taking off into the sky. One long-time resident in the area, driving across the Sugar Creek Bridge about ten o'clock Sunday night, spotted the UFO in the eastern sky and phoned the sighting to this reporter. This is not copy for a society column unless visitors from another planet or from outer space might be accepted as news—if it *is* news. Is it, or isn't it? Any of our readers seen any new UFO's lately—flying box cars, saucers, mobile homes, winged turtles, little green men wearing little green hats?"

Even though I was too sleepy to be angry at what Poetry was reading and at the sarcastic way of writing about what I guessed Dragonfly's mother had maybe reported, it seemed like I wished Dragonfly was right and that we ourselves could actually see a real UFO, 'cause Dragonfly was a member of the gang, and even though we often teased him about his superstitions, we would fight for him any time—kind of like I would fight *with* my sister Charlotte Ann, but also would fight *for* her if anybody else said anything about her or was even one tenth as ornery to her as I sometimes was.

It was still quite awhile before most of the rest of the gang would be there, so I eased myself into Wynken, Blynken and Nod's boat and started to sail away again, letting Nature help me all she could.

Again from beside behind me, Poetry's unwelcome voice broke into my sleep world, as he quoted at me a Bible verse every boy and even every girl in the world ought to know and obey, which was: "Go to the ant, thou sluggard; consider her ways and be wise."

"Go to the ant yourself," I mumbled and drifted away again, getting waked up too soon by the crunchety-crunch-crunch of running footsteps coming from the direction of our house.

Forcing my mind and my eyes open, I saw Little Jim Foote in tan jeans and white T-shirt, trotting along, carrying his striped ash stick which looked like a three-foot-long candy cane without any crook at the top. He'd made the cane, I remembered, by peeling off strips of the gray bark with his scout knife. You hardly ever saw Little Jim without his cane which he was always swinging around, using it to sock different things, whatever he wanted to whenever he wanted to, and sometimes he would kill a snake with it—there being quite a few different kinds of snakes in the territory, especially along the creek and in the swamp. It was also good for reaching up and knocking an apple off a tree, or jabbing into a bumblebee's nest just before you took off on a fast run in some direction or other to get out of the way of maybe thirty-seven angry, black and yellow, long-tongued, sharp-stingered, winged fighters.

Every time I see a bumblebee I remember the fight our gang had with a tough town gang on the slope of Strawberry Hill. That fight had rolled and tumbled itself onto a bumblebees' nest—and almost before we knew it the fight was over. I also remember Dad's strict orders to me and to the gang *not* to kill even one bumblebee because they were needed by the farmers to help pollinate the red clover which can only be pollinated by bees with extra-long tongues.

In a few panting seconds Little Jim had plopped himself down on the ground beside and between Poetry and me. My olfactory nerves came to life when I smelled the flowers. They didn't smell as sweet as Little Jim's mother's perfume. "Where'd you get the black-eyed susans?" I asked him and he answered, "Up by the papaw bushes. I'm going to put 'em on Alexander's grave."

I squinted my eyes at Little Jim's bouquet of black and yellow flowers which he already had in a quart glass jar half-full of water.

Right away there was the crunch-crunch-crunching sound of another boy's feet, running from the direction of the bayou, and almost at the same time a long-tailed sneeze that told us it was the ragweed season and that Dragonfly's hayfever had started. A split second later there was the turtledove's "coo-o, coo-o," and at almost the very same time, the harsh, rattling, grating "kow-kow-kow kuk-kuk" of the rain crow.

Dragonfly was as excited as I had ever seen him, as he came puffing into our circle. "D'you guys hear that? It's Alexander the Coppersmith! He's come to life! My mother heard him last night!"

I straightened up, rested on my elbow, looked that crooked-nosed, excited little member of our gang in his dragonflylike eyes and disagreed, "Dead dogs don't come back to life. What you heard just now was a turtledove and a rain crow doing a duet—not a dead dog howling and barking at the some time from somewhere up in two different trees!"

"My mother heard him last night, down along the bayou, between our cornfield and the swimming hole! I *know* she heard him!"

"*How* do you know?" Circus asked, and Dragonfly gave him a set-jaw look as he answered, " 'Cause my mother has insomnia. She was awake most of the night and heard everything that could be heard, that's why."

"Your mother has *what?*" Poetry cut in to ask, and Dragonfly, maybe thinking he ought to be proud of his mother for having something none of the other gang's mothers had, said, "Insomnia! I-N-S-O-M-N-I-A," spelling the word to let us know he knew how to.

"*Well,*" Poetry said teasingly, "maybe that's why she heard it—anybody with I-N-S-O-M-N-I-A could imagine anything."

That seemed to set Dragonfly's temper on fire, and started him toward Poetry with both fists flying—which maybe Dragonfly ought not to be blamed for, because any boy wouldn't want any other boy to say anything against his mother, even if the other boy was only teasing.

For a few fast-flying jiffies it looked like there might be a fierce, fast fist fight. Dragonfly was like a little wildcat, letting his bony knuckled fists go wham-wham-wham-whop-sock-sock-sock on Poetry's fat sides and stomach and several other places.

The fight had been going on only a few hot-tempered minutes when Big Jim came running up the path that borders the bayou. Seeing and hearing what was going on, he stopped the brawl by grabbing both boys by their collars and yanking them apart. "*What* is going on here!" he demanded.

"He called my mother a bad name," Dragonfly sniffled, trying to break loose to give Poetry's unprotected jaw another sock.

Big Jim kept on holding them apart and told them firmly, "If you really want to fight, we'll set a date, get you some boxing gloves and follow the Marquis of Queensberry rules."

Dragonfly came out with a ridiculous question, then, which was "What's the Queen's berries got to do with it?"

Poetry, still being in a mischievous mood, and being a reader of more books than the rest of us, came out with a saucy answer to his stubborn little opponent: "That's what I say—away back in the nineteenth century John Sholto Douglas, a Marquis of Queensbury, England, helped a boxer named Arthur Chambers write twelve special rules for boxing. They changed it from bare knuckles to gloves, and all fights had to be in three-minute rounds. Does that satisfy you? If it doesn't—"

Poetry was just getting a good start letting Dragonfly, and maybe the rest of us, know what he'd read lately in some encyclopedia, when Big Jim broke in to demand, "What's this fight really about?"

Little Jim started to explain, got interrupted by several of the rest of us, and then at Big Jim's orders told why Dragonfly and Poetry were scuffling, the rest of us keeping our voices out of it.

Say! Do you know what? Big Jim acted like he thought Dragonfly might have a point. "If," he said soberly, "Alexander *is* alive, and *if* he runs and plays at night along the bayou and up in the hills or in the path that goes through the swamp, Dragonfly's mother could have heard him. Let's all be friends again—you two especially—and let's go on up to the cemetery to have a look around. I heard a dog howling last night myself, and it sounded like it was near the mouth of the cave or maybe out in the swamp."

Say, do you know what? When you don't believe something, and a very special friend of yours all of a sudden *does* believe it, it's kind of hard not to change your mind and believe it yourself. I looked at Big Jim's set-jawed face and liked him a lot.

51

"You sure you're not just saying that, so Dragonfly won't feel like a dumb bunny?" I managed to whisper to him so nobody else could hear it.

Big Jim lowered his eyebrows at me and gestured toward Dragonfly with his eyes, and with a smallish jerk of his head.

Knowing Circus' father had three hounds which sometimes made a lot of dog noise at night, I turned to Circus and asked, "Did one of your hounds get out of the kennel last night and go hunting on his own maybe?"

"Not even Silent Sal," Circus answered with a shake of his head. I knew if Silent Sal, one of their best varmint trailers, had treed an animal anywhere, most anybody in the neighborhood would have heard her. She was what is called a "silent trailer," which means that when she is following the trail she never lets out a bark or bawl or squall or howl, but only when her nose has snuffled the coon or possum or skunk or whatever it is, all the way to its hiding place, then she *really* turns loose.

Big Jim still had his eyes on me and his set face told me he didn't exactly like my doubting him, if I did, which I really *didn't*. I was just doubting myself.

"All right," he said firmly, "let's go on up to Alexander's grave and see if he's still buried there."

"I'll bet there'll be a hole in the ground where we buried him," Dragonfly offered.

I quick looked at Little Jim's serious face to see if he was beginning to be scared, but he didn't seem to

52

be, though he was gripping his cane with both hands like he was ready to use it on anything he had to, if he had to.

Before any of the rest of us could say anything further, Big Jim was off and running and calling back over his shoulder, "Come on, everybody! On the double! Follow me!"

Quick as six barefoot flashes, all of us on the double and triple, quadruple, and also *sextuple,* because there were six of us, were running pell-mell in the direction of the sycamore tree, the cave and the swamp.

It's one of the most wonderful experiences ever a boy can have, feeling the soft, green—and sometimes sun-browned—bluegrass carpet under his bare feet as he races plop-plop-ploppety-sizzle through the woods, with his best friends running beside, behind or in front of him, dodging briars, stooping to miss over-hanging branches, being careful not to let any low hanging branch you have pushed aside, fly back and hit the friend behind you in the face—all of you racing helter-skelter toward some kind of adventure, new and exciting and maybe even dangerous.

What would we find when we finally reached the haunted house and sort of crept around it to the cemetery and peeked over the weed-grown fence at the overhanging elderberry, under which just one month age we had buried the most important dog hero in Sugar Creek history?

Chapter 5

In almost no time, it seemed, we reached the rail fence at the west end of the woods, leaped over or crawled under or between the rails, whichever different ones of us decided in a hurry to do, lickety-sizzled ourselves across the graveled road, up the small incline on the other side, through or over or under another rail fence, and went zip-zip-zipping on, following the ridge above the creek until we came to the steep path that leads down to the branch about fifteen feet from where it empties into Sugar Creek.

Right away we were all on the other side of the slow water of the branch—all except me, that is. Because my mother had ordered me to be especially careful of my new denim jeans, I decided to go a little farther upstream and cross on the narrow log bridge there. Being especially careful, and having my eyes also on Little Jim who had leaped across a narrow place and was already clambering up the bank ahead of me, I slipped on a slippery place on the log, lost my balance and landed in about two feet of the wettest water that ever a boy's new blue jeans landed in.

As wet in different places as a drowned rat, I sort of waded up the slippery slope on the other side, and

54

hurried sloshety-sizzle after the gang in the footpath that leads to the sycamore tree, the mouth of the cave and the mysterious trail that leads into and through the swamp.

In maybe eight minutes we came to the place where the path divided—the right fork leading to the syca-more tree and the cave, and the left toward Poetry's place. There we stopped to catch our breath; and there also we *got* stopped because Poetry panted to all of us: "Who's in a hurry to go to a cemetery! That's the last place on earth anybody goes to anyway"—using a very old worn-out joke most people trying to be fun-ny had stopped using years ago. "Let's go see Old Whitey and her family—she's the most popular sow in the country now, getting her picture in the paper, and mostly because she's *my* mother hog, you know," he finished, strutting a little and shaking his head proud-ly like he and not Old Whitey was the most important news in the *Hoosier Graphic*.

To humor our fat friend, we took the left fork and went toward the open-trunked sycamore tree in their barnyard, which tree is as old as the other same-sized sycamore at the mouth of the cave. They'd have made a pair of giant tree twins if they had happened to grow side by side.

I could tell we were getting close to Old Whitey and her litter when Dragonfly began to get a mussed-up expression on his face, stopped, took a jerky deep breath, with his face tilted toward the sky like he was fighting a sneeze. I could feel my own face going into

55

a tailspin too because of my wet clothes and the breeze that was blowing across the barnyard against me.

In another several jiffies we came to within maybe twenty-seven feet of the tree, my nose and my ears telling me we were about to see an old white mother hog with her six little pigs.

Poetry spoke first, saying, "There, Dragonfly, my dear, is your howling dog. A famous mother hog and her family of new pigs. Listen to them squeal! They sound just like a howling dog, wouldn't you say?"

"What my mother heard and saw last night wasn't any old mother hog and her litter of grunting pigs, 'cause six pigs don't sound like one dog howling. Anyway, what she saw skimming through the woods was above the ground, not lying on it. It was snow-white and had green lights that went on and off and—"

"Old Whitey is snow-white," Poetry countered.

I decided to defend Dragonfly, maybe because I liked red mother hogs better than white ones, saying, "You mean she's *supposed* to be white—if only she'd take a bath in anything other than a mud puddle, and sleep in a nice clean modern hog house like any ordinary hog!"

Poetry, in one of his anytime mischievous moods, began quoting a poem to a little singsong tune most of us knew. The poem was:

Six little pigs in the straw with their mother,
Bright eyes, curly tails, tumbling on each other;
Bring them apples from the orchard trees,
And hear those piggies say, "Please, please, please!"

"*Seven* little pigs," Little Jim corrected, counting them again to be sure he was right. "And they're *not* in the *straw!*"

I guess one of the most interesting things a boy ever sees around a farm or ranch is a brand-new pig family having breakfast or dinner or supper, and, as I once heard my father say to Mom when they didn't know I was up in the haymow sort of accidentally listening, "It makes a man believe in God and love Him a little more when he sees how He works in nature."

I never did forget Dad's words, and after that every time we had any kind of newborn life around our place, such as a calf or colt or lamb, and even when all of a sudden some morning I saw five or six baby birds in a nest where the night before there had been five or six eggs, I'd been saying—sort of half to myself and half to God—"It makes a man believe in God and love Him a little more."

Right that second while the gang was being entertained by those wriggling, bright-eyed, curly-tailed, pinkish-white little squealers, I was remembering what Dad had said to Mom, and for some reason a very glad feeling splashed into my mind, making me want to leap up and catch hold of an overhanging branch of the ash sapling I was standing beside and under, which also right that minute I did. I chinned myself three times, swung myself up and over, doing what is called skinning the cat.

While I was upside down, looking at the upside-down pigs and their mother in their tree house, Poetry said again, "Your howling dog *was* our Old Whitey! Now are you satisfied, Dragonfly, my friend?"

Circus answered Poetry's idea by correcting him, saying, "Howling dogs don't squeal and squealing pigs don't howl."

"Besides," Dragonfly whined, ignoring Circus' correction, "the dog my mother heard last night was copper-colored and this old mother hog is a dirty white."

"How did she know it was copper-colored? You can't even see copper color in the dark. Anyway, I thought you said it was a *white* dog!"

Dragonfly's face went into a tailspin like he was about to sneeze again, then it went set and he answered, "It *had* to be copper-colored 'cause that's the color Alexander the Coppersmith is."

"*Was,*" I put in. "Ghosts are white, you know—or don't you?"

Well, we weren't getting anywhere trying to change anybody's mind, so we decided to leave the seven little pigs in the straw—or whatever it was they were tumbling in—and go on up to the cemetery like we had planned, to let Little Jim put the flowers on the grave, and also to let Dragonfly see for himself that the mound of yellowish-brown earth was still there just as we had left it a month ago—only of course there'd be a few weeds growing on it, and maybe some wild grass or dandelions.

As we ambled along, I happened to think that if there were a dozen or more dandelions in the cemetery, I could dig a few of them with my knife and take them back to our place to see if I could sell them for a cent apiece to Dad. Well, I could *try* to sell them anyway.

Even though I knew there wouldn't be any hole in the ground under the elderberry bush, it seemed like I was wondering if there would be, and almost *hoping* there would be.

Little Jim, I noticed, was gripping his cane as if he would be ready to use it to defend himself if we did run onto a ghost—either animal or human. He was still carrying the bouquet of black-eyed susans in his left hand, and every now and then as we pell-melled ourselves along beside, behind and in front of each other, I caught a whiff of their scent—it wasn't one of the sweetest flower smells in the whole world.

After maybe seventeen minutes of speeding along, part of the time almost like six little pigs tumbling on each other—*stumbling*, though, not tumbling—we came to within sight of the haunted house, which is the thick-walled stone house that had once been the home of Old Tom the Trapper who many years ago had gotten shot through the heart with an Indian arrow. There, all of a scary sudden, we stopped, because again, as clear as a school bell on an early September morning, we heard from above—or from in front or behind us, we couldn't tell for sure—the long, eerie wailing squall of some kind of animal.

"*It's him!*" Dragonfly cried. "I knew it! It's his

ghost! My mother was right! Come on, everybody, let's go see the empty grave!"

Twelve flying bare feet racing toward the old stone house and the canine cemetery behind it—that was us. Running like that, so fast and almost blindly, somebody in a gang of boys is bound to stumble over something, which right then, Little Jim did. Reaching out to try to stop himself from falling too hard, his bouquet of black-eyed susans flew out of his hand, and it took several nervous minutes for him to gather them up again—the rest of the gang not stopping, because Little Jim and I were behind them, and maybe they didn't know what had happened.

As you probably remember, Little Jim was the only one of the gang who sometimes talked with me about things in the Bible, maybe because he thought I was his best friend, which maybe I was. So, while I was helping him pick up his scattered flowers, he said, "There won't *be* any dogs in heaven; my mother just read in the Bible where it was talking about heaven, and it says, '*Without* are dogs.' "

I shook off a half-dozen black carpenter ants which I had picked up with one of the flower showers of a black-eyed susan stalk, part of his bouquet having landed on a dead half-rotten log, the very log Little Jim had stumbled over in the first place. "Where'd she read that in the Bible—what verse?" I asked, as we took off after the gang, and he panted back an answer, "Revelation 22:15. She read it this morning."

Our feet were plop-plopping faster and faster as we

60

raced after the gang, trying to catch up with them. "Maybe it doesn't mean animal dogs," I said over my shoulder to him. "Maybe it means people dogs—people who keep their hearts' doors shut against the Saviour, and maybe wouldn't even enjoy heaven if they got there—unless they got their hearts changed before they died"—having heard our pastor say something like that himself once in a sermon.

We caught up with the gang just as they reached the cemetery fence. The first thing I noticed as we stood panting and sweating and looking in, was the mound of yellow earth, and at the end of it, Little Jim's headstone that said:

ALEXANDER THE COPPERSMITH
Long may he live in our hearts.

There wasn't any hole in the ground like the kind a butterfly or moth leaves when it changes from a caterpillar, crawls out of its cocoon and flies away.

"See there," Poetry said to Dragonfly with a sharp arrow in his voice, "he's still buried down there, two feet deep, so nobody could have heard him last night."

"How come we all heard him ourselves in broad daylight less than ten minutes ago?" Big Jim surprised us all with.

Dragonfly was staring at the overhanging flower shower of the elderberry and it seemed like he was going to cry, 'cause he was sniffling a little, but I should have known better 'cause the weeds lining the fence were ragweeds in full pollen, and right away our crooked-nosed little guy let out a high-pitched, long-tailed sneeze like he likes to do—maybe to get attention.

Poetry came in then with a sarcastic "Now that *did* sound like a howling dog howling!"

"Ragweeds!" Dragonfly exclaimed. "Let's get out of here!"

I'd already seen them—a whole fencerow of them, with their deeply lobed leaves; and without being allergic to them myself, I could tell that the air was already heavy with the thousands of sharp-edged pollen grains—which any boy who is going to be a doctor some day knows is the way ragweed pollen grains are, even though you'd have to use a microscope to see how sharp they *really* are.

As soon as Little Jim had set his bouquet where he'd set it before—in a quart jar he had filled from the old wooden pump near the house—we went into the house through the secret entrance we knew about through the cellar door, just to sort of look around a little like we nearly always do when we're there.

We were maybe all thinking different things about the exciting things that had happened there—such as the one you read about in the story *Down a Sugar Creek Chimney,* and in the one called *The Haunted House at Sugar Creek.* It was a kind of dreary place today, so we pretty soon went outside into the sunlit woods, all of us still feeling sad because, in spite of Poetry's mischievous mood, we were all thinking seriously about things. I myself was remembering Little

Jim's quoted Bible verse about heaven which says, "Without are dogs."

In a little while we were at the farther edge of the woods and at the beginning of the path that skirts the swamp. There Dragonfly helped us decide to take the shortcut to Old Man Paddler's cabin by going *through* the swamp. "We might see a man from Mars, or some other planet, like my mother says was driving the flying saucer last night. There was a UFO *above* the swamp at the same time Alexander was howling."

Hearing that serious-faced little member of our gang say that like that, I knew he hadn't given up his belief, so I said, "OK, gang, let's do it! Maybe we *will* see a little green man from Mars."

The rest of the gang decided it was a good idea, especially since we *did* want to go past Old Man Paddler's vacant cabin, so we swung into the path and were soon ambling along in one of the coolest places in the whole territory, going right past the place where once we had seen a big old mother bear wallowing in the mud—which fierce old mad mother bear Little Jim himself had shot with Big Jim's rifle, which you know about in the story *We Killed a Bear*.

Pretty soon we reached the grassy knoll near the muskrat pond where I remembered Alexander had had his underwater battle with the savage-mandibled mud turtle half as big in diameter as a large washtub, when all of a mysterious sudden, and from so close to my ear it made me jump, Dragonfly hissed, "Sh-h! Somebody's coming!"

Chapter 6

THE MINUTE DRAGONFLY scared us with his hissing, we stopped stock-still and stared, then took a hurried look in a quick circle of directions—and Dragonfly was right. In the winding path ahead, somebody *was* coming—a man or woman, or maybe a girl, we couldn't tell for sure at first.

The man or woman or girl was carrying what looked like a traveling man's attaché case and also a camera.

Big Jim took charge of us by hissing, "Down, everybody!"

And down we dropped, sheltering ourselves behind a drift from last spring's heavy rains that had made the creek overflow the bayou and Dragonfly's dad's cornfield. It had piled up in quite a few different places—large drifts of cornstalks and straw from barnyards and fields upstream. Behind one of those drifts we were now crouching, tense and waiting—I in my wet clothes, thinking that when the rest of the gang stood up, they could just dust off their clothes and they'd be as clean as any boy can make them for inspection by his parents; but I, Bill Collins, whose mother had ordered me to be careful, would be covered with damp dirt you couldn't just brush off.

"What're we hiding from?" Poetry wanted to know.

Big Jim turned to shush him, saying in a tense whisper, "I don't know yet—not till we find out who it is and what he is doing."

"What she is doing, you mean. It's a girl," Circus said, he having six sisters and maybe knowing better than any of the rest of us what a girl looked like.

"How can you tell this far away?" Poetry asked.

"Circus is right," I answered, peeking through a crack in the edge of the drift. "She's wearing gray slacks, a bright red blouse, a Western-style belt, sunglasses and wading boots."

Some one of us must have made too much noise right then 'cause Big Jim waved his hand behind him for us to keep still, which, for a few tense seconds most of us managed to do, it being maybe as hard on a boy's nerves to have to keep still as it is on his mother's nerves when he doesn't—as Dad sometimes says, "It's good for a tired-out mother and a nervous, fidgety child to get away from each other every once in a while."

Say, that girl in the gray slacks, red blouse and wading boots was certainly acting mysterious. It looked like she was trying to sneak up on something at or near or in the muskrat pond.

Poetry, whose face was close to my ear, whispered, "Look! She's set her briefcase down! She's got her camera and is going to take a picture of something."

My eyes were seeing what he was seeing. She was creeping closer and closer to the cottonwood log that runs from the shore about seventeen feet out into the pond.

65

Dragonfly, whose face was close to my other ear, and who was trying to look through the same crack in the drift I was looking through, whispered, "She's balancing herself on the log." And she was, easing herself along, getting slowly closer and closer to the end, out where the water was deeper, and where also, about ten feet from the *very* end, was an old raft we boys had made and left there, and on that raft were about nine soft-shelled turtles taking an afternoon sunbath.

My wet clothes were like a boy's voice in my mind, making me want to call out to her, "Look, lady! Be careful. That log's slippery! Any second, you'll step on something slimy, and down you'll go!" But I made myself keep still.

She raised her camera now, focused it on the raft and the turtles, just as Poetry whispered, "It's a *movie* camera!" which made me think that if it had a zoom lens and a color film, she'd be getting a picture of one of nature's finest sights—a closeup of nine or maybe ten or twelve spiny, soft-shelled turtles which, as any boy around Sugar Creek knows, are olive-green in color, with a narrow yellow border all the way around. When a spiny, soft-shelled turtle is still young and not more than ten inches in diameter, its green carapace is spotted all over with black rings the size of a boy's big toenail.

It would certainly be something to see it in a color picture, if all of a sudden those nine turtles would wake up, scramble into turtle life and take nine nose dives in nine different directions into and under the water, which turtles nearly always do whenever anything startles them.

As you maybe know, turtle's feet are like fins, which help make them some of nature's best skin divers.

I'd no sooner thought that than it began to happen—they *did* wake up scared and began to make nine four-legged scrambles for the water trying to get away from what they maybe thought was some terrible red-bloused monster about to murder them and make turtle soup out of them. If turtles could think and talk to each other, once they were safe under the water, one of the smallest turtles might say to his mother, "Did you see her three big eyes?" And his mother could answer, "What three eyes?" And her turtle husband might answer, "Two in her head and another great big one on the end of her long right fin."

Anyway, one of the smallest turtles was in such a hurry to get away from what he maybe thought was some terrible danger, that he got tangled up in the maddish rush for the water, upped himself on top of the carapace of another larger, awkward-moving turtle, tumbled off onto the raft, and for a second was upside down, waving his excited fins in the air, giving us —and the camera—a glimpse of his snowy white plastron, almost as white as the front of one of Dad's dress shirts.

I was just thinking up a joke for Dragonfly when something else began to happen—the girl began to lose her balance.

It was in my mind to say to Dragonfly, "There, my friend, is your flying saucer—nine of them in fact; green just like the ones your mother said she saw last night, and their undersides are a clean, white white."

When you are wearing wading boots, trying to balance yourself on a slippery cottonwood log no wider than thirteen inches, it's easier to lose your balance than it is to keep it. A certain all-wet boy I know, knows.

In less time than it would take me to tell it, and almost as fast as it took me to *think* it, the girl in the gray slacks and red blouse did lose her balance, her arms with a camera in one hand waving in a dozen excited directions of up and down and sidewise. Then ker-splashety-plop, she was off the end of the log and into the water—red blouse, silver-gray slacks, wading boots, brown hair, pretty face and all—almost all, I mean, she being careful to hold her camera up so it wouldn't get wet.

"What if she can't swim!" Dragonfly worried out loud.

"She won't have to," I answered. "The water's only about four feet deep there!"

Still holding her camera high enough to keep it from getting wet, the girl looked around to get her bearing, then started toward the shore, which was in our direction.

It was a little disappointing at first that we didn't get to rescue a helpless girl, that she seemed as much at home in a muskrat pond as a boy would have been.

68

No sooner had she sloshed her way up the gravelly bank, than she rewound her camera and began looking around for something else interesting and alive to take a picture of. I watched her inch her way toward an overhanging willow whose lacy green branches extended about ten feet out over the water. Creeping up slowly, she started her camera again toward three or four water snakes basking there in the dappled sunlight.

Seeing those savage-looking water snakes reminded me that there are maybe a dozen different kinds of snakes living in our neighborhood, some of them being friends of a farmer or rancher and only a few being dangerous. Some of the friendly ones that won't hurt a boy or even a fly if they don't happen to like to eat flies, are the hognose snakes like the one you read about in *Lost in a Sugar Creek Blizzard,* and the innocent garter snakes which eat fishing worms, snails, small frogs, small mice and other stuff a boy wouldn't eat anyway. Maybe I never told you that every autumn about thirty garter snakes get together in a garter snake family reunion on Strawberry Hill near the cemetery where Old Man Paddler's wife and two boys are buried. When the days are warm those innocent snakes warm themselves in the sun, then at night crawl into burrows and clefts in the rocky places and sleep late every morning like a schoolboy would do every Saturday if his parents or baby sister would let him. Then when a hard freeze comes and kills the leaves on the trees and spreads the frost, those easy-going garter snakes go underground for the winter.

Another kind of snake around Sugar Creek is the blue racer, which has a greenish-blue back and a pale yellow stomach and sometimes gets to be four or five feet long. Once in a while there is a rattlesnake, and in the swamp now and then we spot a savage water moccasin, which is sometimes as long as five feet and eats frogs, fish, small rabbits and even rats.

The girl was working her way closer and closer to our hiding place now, and any minute she might find out we were there. If all of a sudden she discovered six boys, one of them all wet and caked with mud, it might startle her worse than a rattlesnake might.

All of a startling sudden, Circus let out a yell, grabbed Little Jim's cane, sprang out of our hiding place, streaked toward the girl who had her back turned to a small water puddle and didn't see what Circus saw and what none of the rest of us saw until later.

"Look out!" Circus half-screamed as he ran. "There's a water moccasin behind you, ready to strike!"

Like a streak of curly-headed lightning our acrobat raced toward the girl, getting there almost before anybody could think that fast, and began flailing away with Little Jim's cane on the inch-and-a-half-wide head and two-inches-in-diameter body of what looked like a five-foot-long water moccasin, the most poisonous snake in our territory, except for maybe the rattlesnake which always warns before it strikes, though sometimes there are not more than a few seconds between the rattling noise and the savage strike-strike-strike.

I knew a water moccasin warns you with its tail also, but not with a rattling noise. When you accidentally surprise one or wake him out of his nap, he draws his ugly head back, lifts it ready to strike, opens his mouth wide enough for the white parts to show—which is why a water moccasin is sometimes called a cottonmouth. Then he shakes his tail—not like a friendly dog wagging his, but in angry back-and-forth jerks—which is the snake's way of shouting, "I hate you. I hate you and I'm going to kill you!" Then if you are still close enough for it to strike and it is still angry at you or maybe afraid you are going to hurt it, it *will* strike savagely, and you'd better not be in the way and you'd better not have bare feet or legs.

If the moccasin *doesn't* strike, after a few jiffies of glaring at you with his beady eyes as if you were a saber-toothed tiger, it might decide to just glide away, as much as to say, "So what! You're only a human being, and not fit for a fine snake like me!"

But this moccasin must have hated girls, or maybe her red blouse made him see red. *Before* Circus got there, I saw that savage-headed, heavy-bodied, brown-backed, yellow-stomached, beady-eyed, fierce-fanged water moccasin which carried deadly poison in its cotton-mouthed mouth, strike twice at the girl's ankles.

71

Chapter 7

TALK ABOUT FAST ACTION. Circus' racing toward that cottonmouth, getting there in nothing flat, and smashing that fierce-fanged water moccasin's ugly head flatter'n a pancake, was like a copper-colored dog leaping into action to save Little Jim from being killed by a wildcat.

Wham, wham, sock, sock and double-wham! Little Jim's cane, in the strong-muscled hands of our acrobat, rose and fell, rose and fell, rose and fell! Instead of what *might* have happened, what *did* happen was as cheerful as one of Mom's happiness breaks. Instead of that ugly water moccasin's two poisonous fangs burying themselves deep in the girl's ankle and holding on like the cottonmouth's fangs do when they strike a small rabbit or fish or bird or frog until the victim dies—I say, *instead* of what *might* have happened— something wonderful did. Several things, in fact, happened.

The girl's face did blanch and she looked scared, but only for a few seconds, as she looked quick at her booted ankles where the snake had struck, then she said to Circus, "Thank you, sir. Thank you very, *very* much. If I hadn't been wearing these clumsy old boots—thanks to my father—when I was just going to wear my casuals because I thought the weather was too hot for boots— Excuse me." She cut her sentence off and flew into fast action, focused her camera on the writhing, dying snake as it twisted and turned, coiled and uncoiled, then rolled over on its dark back, exposing its yellow stomach with its blotched brown and black markings.

We were all out of our hiding place behind the drift now, watching the girl take the picture of the dying moccasin, and I was wondering different things, such as who was she and why was she taking the pictures, also how come she didn't act more scared—at least as much as a boy might have been. Then as clear as a church bell ringing on Sunday morning calling all the Sugar Creek boys and their families to hurry up or they'd be late, we heard from somewhere deep in the swamp—or maybe from the other side near the wooded area below Old Man Paddler's cabin—the ghostly long-toned trembling squall of an animal of some kind.

That trembling-voiced howl couldn't have been Circus Brown imitating a loon or a howling dog, 'cause he was right beside us, and the sound I had just heard had come from quite a distance away. It wasn't a screech owl, nor a rain crow and turtledove duet. It was—I was absolutely sure—an honest-to-goodness howling dog.

Seven times as fast as a turtle tumbling off a log raft into the water, the girl with the camera gave three

73

sharp, shrill blasts with a whistle she had on a string around her neck and turned to say to us, to Circus especially: "Thank you again, very, *very* much. If Old Moccasin had had a chance to strike a third time, he might have struck *above* my boot tops. I knew he was here somewhere and I'd been trying to get a good picture of him, but always he'd slither away before I could get focused on him. Father will be so pleased with the picture I did get."

My eyes and mind were still on the twisting, writhing, still-dying water moccasin, so I was startled again by the long-toned wailing squall of some kind of animal—alive in his own body, or dead without one.

A sound like that when you are in a swamp, cringing beside a dying snake, not even able to believe what you are seeing and hearing anyway, can give you a scary feeling.

"It's time for me to start supper," the girl in the red blouse said. She turned, picked up the attaché case and started off toward the direction the sound had sounded like it had come from; then she stopped, turned back to us and said with a friendly voice, "Father and I are camping in the aspen grove at the Seneth Paddler place. You must come to see us while we're here. I think my father will have a reward for you, sir," she finished with her eyes on Circus.

Hearing another squall from whatever it was, a coyote or some other animal, she broke into a run, and a few seconds later disappeared in the little brown winding path that leads to the woods below Old Man

Paddler's cabin, leaving six boys to wonder what on earth and why, because of the UFO's which people had been talking about lately.

For maybe a hundred seconds, we kept as quiet as six scared mice hiding from a hungry cat, then Big Jim broke the silence with a husky question. "Tell me," he began, "*did* we or *didn't* we see a girl taking a picture of nine turtles on a raft, then losing her balance and falling off into the water; and *did* we or *didn't* we kill a water moccasin that would have scared any ordinary girl half to death?"

Dragonfly joined in with another question: "D-didn't we or did we h-hear Alexander the Coppersmith alive like my mother said?"

I rubbed my eyes to see if I was awake, thinking maybe I'd only dreamed what I'd seen and heard, and pretty soon would wake up and find myself lying in the shade of the beechnut tree near the Black Widow Stump, listening to the hum and buzz of seven hundred honeybees working the creamy yellow flowers of the leaning linden tree.

One look at the two-inch-in-diameter, five-foot-long water moccasin with a bashed-in head from Little Jim's cane, convinced me that I had not been dreaming—unless maybe I *really* was, and only *thought* I had seen the snake.

Little Jim helped bring me back to reality, when he took the cane, eased himself down to the edge of the pond and began swishing it in the water to get the blood off the end.

"Listen!" Dragonfly cried excitedly. "There he is again!"

As sure as anything—and maybe still surer—from a long distance away, there came once more the long, lonely wail of the ghost dog—if it was a ghost, and if it was a dog—and a second later a sharp, shrill blast from the girl's whistle.

We couldn't stay all the rest of the afternoon where we were, as our parents might start worrying—and for a boy there isn't anything worse than a worrying parent, even when there isn't anything to worry about. He tries to keep from doing things that will cause them to worry, and *if* they are already worrying, he will go whistling around the place doing things to help squeeze all the worry out of them, such as speeding up the outdoor chores, or offering to help with the housework without being told to—Mom doing most of her out-loud worrying when she is tired or doesn't feel well, and needs her first and worst son to prove he loves her.

For Theodore Collin's first and worst son, his jeans still soiled with swamp dust, on his way home from an afternoon's happiness break, there might be a little worrying he himself would have to do. In fifteen or twenty minutes I'd find out.

The first thing I saw when I came through the orchard gate—coming home the back way instead of through the front gate by our mailbox—was Mixy near the grape arbor giving herself a bath with her damp, rough tongue.

"You been wallowing in the barnyard dust?" I said down to her, and she looked up at me with smoky green eyes, meowed a lazy meow, then went back to her bath.

It gave me an idea, though—her giving herself a licking like that. I quick went to the tool shed, came out with the beech switch in my right hand, went around to the front door of our house where company or salesmen nearly always come first, and knocked on the screen door. By the time Mom could get to the door from some other part of the house, I was ready for her. I was going to try a little playacting like Mom and I sometimes do when we are together.

Mom had one of the nicest company faces a mother ever had, also one of the nicest company *voices*, which made it especially cheerful at our house when anybody came—and also, made company want to come back, "sometimes too soon," Dad sometimes told her. So when I looked through the screen door and saw her grayish-brown hair, her soft brown friendly eyes, I hurried to say, "Good afternoon, Madam, I've come to report an accident. Your son fell into the water near the mouth of the branch, and then while he was hiding from a girl wearing a red blouse and taking pictures of a dying snake that had been killed by Little Jim's cane, just before a dog howled, he got himself covered with dust from the drift he was hiding behind with the gang. Would you be interested in buying a beech switch to use on him?'"

Mom had opened her mouth several times to try

to get a word in edgewise, and couldn't until I had finished my fast-talking speech, then she said in as calm a voice as I had ever heard her use, "I get everything but the drift. But whatever happened, you're still my son. There's so much work to be done before supper I won't have time to be interested in anything made out of beech wood."

"Could I interest you in anything else? I have several marbles."

"I'm sorry," Mom answered, "but this is Saturday, and we have shopping to do tonight."

"Nothing?" I said through the screen door to her.

She said, "Nothing at all. But my dear man, if you'd like to earn your supper, you can go gather the eggs. Excuse me, sir. There's the phone."

As Mom went to answer the telephone which was on the wall by the east window of the living room, I turned, sighed a happy sigh, and listened to see if I could tell by the tone of voice she was using and the things she was saying, who had called.

I *could* tell, before she'd said maybe seven words, because I heard her say, "I know the papers are full of it, but—"

It was Lucy Gilbert, Dragonfly's mother, I thought, worried about all the talk there was in the country and the news in the news about flying saucers, and she was doing what maybe seventeen different women in Mom's Sunday school class did when they had a worry to worry about—they called Mom who was their teacher to ask questions and to help get rid of the

78

troubles that had been building crows' nests in their minds.

I guess maybe there never was a better mother than mine, I thought, as I went around the house to stand a few minutes below and beside that east window to hear what Mom was saying. I got there just in time to hear:

"But a mother can't punish a boy every time he makes a mistake. If I were you, Lucy, I'd just ignore it. It was his day for a happiness break, and why should you spoil his fun? Just give him a little more love and I'm sure he won't be so nervous. Our pastor is going to preach on 'The Man from Outer Space' tomorrow, and maybe he'll clear up a lot of things for us."

As I came out of the tool shed, after carefully laying the unneeded beech switch across the gunrack just below Dad's twelve-gauge double-barreled shotgun, I noticed Mixy had finished her bath and was out by the garden fence, having fun catching grasshoppers. I called to her, but she ignored me, not seeming to be interested in anything but herself and in doing what she wanted to do.

There was such a warm feeling in my heart because my mother had been so kind, had acted like my accident of falling off a log into the water was only a mistake, and on the phone was trying to keep Dragonfly's mother from being too anxious about her nervous, worrywart son, Roy, and also from worrying about whether the world was coming to an end because of

79

all the things people had been seeing in the night sky. I say, there was such a warm feeling that it seemed like I ought to tell God something very special when I got to the barn and would be all by myself up in the haymow looking for eggs.

Just then the screen door behind me slammed, and it was Charlotte Ann, coming on the run, carrying her small sand bucket, wanting to go with me to help gather the eggs.

At the iron pitcher pump I stopped and pumped her a drink in her own special tin cup that hung on a wire hook there. And when she was halfway through drinking, she did with the rest of the water what she'd seen me do maybe a half-hundred times that summer —tossed it over the iron kettle below the pump's spout where it landed with a splash in a three-foot-diameter water puddle there, scattering the daylights out of seventeen or more white and sulphur butterflies that had been there getting a drink.

Say, that is one of the prettiest sights ever a boy or girl sees—a flock of butterflies taking off into the air in all the directions of up that there are, and then coming floating down like more than that many feathers out of a pillow, and settling again in a little circle around the place where they had been drinking.

I watched the white and yellow action, then said to those friendly little butterflies, "If I had wings like you, I could fly across a branch without getting wet."

Later in the haymow I climbed up over the alfalfa to my secret praying place, took the New Testament

80

with Psalms out of its crack in the log where I kept it, and opened it to a special place where I had a bookmark, and where a favorite verse was underlined which was: "Create in me a clean heart, O God."

My prayer with actual words was pretty short because I heard Charlotte Ann fussing at the bottom of the haymow ladder because she wanted to come up and I had told her she couldn't. It sounded like she was actually halfway up. On the way to the ladder, I finished my prayer, part of which was: "And help me to act like a boy who wants to live with a clean heart."

When I looked down and saw my smallish sister already on the third rung, it was hard to act like that kind of boy, but by not yelling down at her, she didn't get scared, lose her balance and fall and crack her crown like Jack did in the poem called "Jack and Jill."

As we went side by side across the barnyard toward the henhouse to look for more eggs, I felt as clean inside as a school of minnows swimming upstream in the riffle that sings along under the branch bridge. Even though I had been an honest-to-goodness-for-sure Christian for quite a few years, it seemed like every now and then I needed to have my heart washed all over again, because I kept accidentally getting it stained in some way.

Right then Mixy, spotting Charlotte Ann's sand pail and my egg basket, must have decided we had something for her to eat. She came loping from somewhere or other toward us, meowing up at us as much as if to say, "If you don't give me something to eat or drink, I'll starve to death!"

"Listen, cat," I said down to her, "you have nine lives. If one of them starves to death this afternoon, you have eight more to go on! Now, scat!"

Mixy was up on her hind legs sniffing at my egg basket when a swallowtail butterfly came loping past. Like a four-legged flash with a bushy tail, she whirled, took off after it, and I went on toward the chicken house, my kid sister holding onto my left little finger with her small chubby right hand, giving me one of the finest feelings ever a brother can have.

Even though I felt clean in my heart and liked my sister a lot, I was also a little worried. What, I wondered, was going on in the world—maybe something different than had ever gone on before. What *were* the different-shaped brightly colored things people were seeing in the sky at night? And what would our minister say about a man from outer space when he preached his sermon tomorrow?

Who was the girl with the red blouse and gray slacks? Why was she taking pictures of the wildlife in the swamp, and what was making the ghostly sound of a howling dog in the swamp and along the bayou?

Chapter 8

NEXT DAY, being Sunday, the Collins family was up as early as on any weekday, flying around to get the outside chores done, breakfast over, the dishes washed and dried. Our Sunday clothes were on, including my shoes which I'd shined two days before. Dad's whiskers were shaved. Mom's face was fixed a little so it wouldn't shine too much from hurrying around too much on what was going to be a hot day. Charlotte Ann's hair was combed and brushed and tied with a ribbon to keep it from getting gone with the wind even before we could get in the car. And in plenty of time we were on our way, zooming up the road as fast as Mom would let Dad drive.

I was in the front seat with Dad. Mom was in the back trying to keep Charlotte Ann from acting her age, when I decided to come out with a question I had asked my parents before but hadn't had an answer to:

"Has anybody found out yet whether there is a special heaven for dogs? Do they go racing up and down the creek at night, bawling on a coon trail or some other varmint like maybe Alexander—"

Dad chopped my question in two by saying, "I

thought you boys went up to put flowers on his grave yesterday. He was still buried there, wasn't he?"

"His *body* still was," I answered.

"Of all *things*!" Mom burst out with. "Did you see that! That woman driver almost ran into us head on!"

"Not a woman," Dad disagreed. "He just had long hair. Didn't you see his beard?"

Something went wrong in the back seat right then, somebody's first and worst daughter letting out a squawk like a young rooster learning to crow.

"She bumped her head on the door handle when you swerved to miss that woman driver," Mom explained.

"*Beatnik* driver," Dad said.

Remembering Little Jim's verse "Without are dogs," I quoted it to Dad and added, "If any dog deserved to go to dog's heaven, it would be Alexander the Coppersmith."

Mom sighed and broke in with something I'd heard our minister say quite a few times, which was: "Even we human beings don't go to heaven because we deserve it, but we are saved because of the grace of God, through faith." Then Mom added, "If anybody *did* get to heaven because he had done so many good things, he'd probably spend part of eternity bragging on himself."

Dad answered Mom's kind of bright remark by saying, "Which would be like a dog chasing himself up a tree, and barking down to everybody below, 'Look! I'm a very clever canine, don't you think?' "

Then Dad's voice took on a teachery tone like it gets when he is giving a talk on nitrogen on alfalfa roots to a farm convention, as he began to explain what Revelation 22:15 means: "That very solemn Bible verse is talking about persons who, because of their stubborn rebellion against God and decency, reject the Saviour. They are the dogs who will be on the outside. When anyone closes his heart against the love of God, he is automatically closing the door to heaven against himself."

In a little while we swished down a shaded hill, rattled across Wolf Creek bridge, started up the incline on the other side, and right away we came to and turned into the church's driveway.

As soon as we were parked in the shade of a spreading elm tree beside the Thompsons' auto, Poetry came around to my side of the car before I could get out and whispered excitedly, "Guess what!"

"What?" I asked, beginning to get that happy feeling I nearly always get when he says, "Guess what!" or "I tell you what let's do!"

"I have something wonderful to tell you. Remember Old Whitey's picture in the *Hoosier Graphic?*"

I wasn't exactly glad to be reminded of it, because it seemed like a red mother hog with seven little wrigglers would have made a better picture. "What's so wonderful about it?" I asked.

"That picture woke up the State Farm Bureau to

the fact that Sugar Creek raises wonderful hogs, and they phoned my father last night to come to Indianapolis for the convention tomorrow. They want to introduce him to all those people and have him make a speech."

"It's Old Whitey who ought to be introduced," I said to my friend. "She's the one who is raising those dirty little off-white pigs."

Poetry frowned at my innocent remark, but went on with what he had wanted to tell me in the first place. "Because Dad has to leave right after dinner and will be gone all night, and because he wants to give me a happiness break, he's going to let you stay all night and sleep in the tent with me. My mother's already asked your mother, and she's already said it's all right."

Dragonfly, seeing us talking and maybe not wanting to be left out of any secrets, came hurrying over from their car which had just stopped and parked, so Poetry and I had to start whistling a tune of some kind and begin talking about the weather, not wanting him to feel jealous if he didn't get to sleep in the tent too.

"My mother heard him again last night," Dragonfly told us, "and she saw another flying saucer above the Sugar Creek island."

The Sunday school bell rang then, and all the people who were still outside stopped visiting and moved toward the double-door entrance of the church. Just as Poetry and I reached the top of the stone steps, he whispered, "If the dog howls again tonight, and if

86

there *is* a flying saucer, I'm going to take its picture. I bought a new roll of color film last night."

Even though I had that to think about during Sunday school and all through the sermon that followed, I did hear most everything our kind-voiced pastor said about "The Man from Outer Space." One of the most important things which seemed extra-wonderful for a boy to know was: "Our Saviour did not *begin* as a little baby in the manger at Bethlehem. *He always was.* He came from heaven, and only went *through* Bethlehem on His way to the cross to die for our sins. After His death, He rose again and ascended into heaven and some day He will come back to our planet again, like He said. *Until* He comes, we are to be busy serving Him."

I wasn't sure what a boy my age could do for Him, but it seemed like I ought to try to be a better boy, be a little kinder to my family, especially to my smallish sister, Charlotte Ann, and I might help Mom and Dad around the place without being told two or three times. Also I ought not to make fun of anybody, even Dragonfly who was superstitious because his mother was. And besides, I thought, as I sat beside the open church window listening to the sermon and every now and then to a meadowlark's juicy notes from the cemetery fence about a hundred yards away, Dragonfly might be right. What if there were actual UFO's flying around? What if there *were* visitors from outer space? What if some of the things people were seeing or thought they were seeing—whichever it was—what if God was letting them happen to kinda scare people a little into behaving themselves and maybe getting their hearts ready for the time when the Man from outer space would come back?

Different thoughts came fast and went fast into and out of my mind. One kind of wonderful thought seemed most important. It was *when the Saviour does come, I won't have to be scared because He and I are already good friends.*

In the car again on our way home, as we went rattling across Wolf Creek bridge, I looked out the window to my right and saw three or four saucer-shaped, soft-shelled turtles sunning themselves on a log which, the minute the bridge's board floor and steel rafters began to rattle and to shake, came to awkward turtle life and slithered off into the water. Even before we reached the other side of the bridge, one of the turtles had swum under water maybe ten feet and come up again for air.

A very quiet, very glad feeling began to swim around in my mind right then because I happened to think that the same heavenly Father who made all the wild things of the world, and maybe loved them a lot because of the way He had taught them to take care of themselves, had also loved human beings even more, and had given His Son, our very own Saviour who liked boys, to die for their sins.

Without knowing I was going to do it, I took a deep breath, sighed like I had just come up for air, and began humming a line of the song we had just sung at the closing of the church service:

> "Take my life and let it be
> Consecrated, Lord, to Thee."

Mom in the back seat heard me sort of sigh the words and asked, "Did you say something, Bill?"

"Did you see the way those soft-shelled flying saucers took off from the raft back there?" I answered her.

Dad came in then with "I'll bet all the little minnows down under the water thought their world was being invaded." Then, reaching the crest of the hill, he stepped on the gas, and we went zooming toward the Collins place, while my thoughts flew on ahead to what might happen tonight in the tent. What if we heard the dog howling in the swamp again? What'd we do? What if when we got up and went out and down to where it sounded like the howling would be coming from—what if we got an actual color picture of it? Or even of a UFO of some kind? *If* we did, it'd be maybe the first honest-to-goodness picture of one that anybody in the world ever saw!

* * *

That afternoon while I was packing my things in Mom's overnight case, the phone rang, and it was Poetry's mother asking if they could borrow two of our muskrat traps.

"How come?" I exclaimed to Mom, astonished that

any boy's mother would want a muskrat trap when it was of season to trap muskrats.

Mom at the phone shushed me by waving her hand behind her and giving me a motherly scowl at the same time.

"Surely," Mom said into the mouthpiece of our phone. "He'll be glad to bring them."

Even though I was itching to find out what the Thompsons wanted muskrat traps for in the middle of the out-of-season, I didn't get to find out until maybe twenty-seven minutes later, during which extra-long time I waited patiently for Mom to keep on talking and listening to Poetry's mother until like an eight-day clock, one of them ran down.

After finishing talking and listening and finally hanging up, Mom said to me, "Some varmint has been getting into their chicken house and she's already lost two of her best laying hens. You're to take over our two traps when you go."

I told Mom what most any farm or ranch boy knows: "But muskrats don't raid anybody's chicken yard. They eat vegetables, crawfish, and any other kind of fish they can catch, and mussels, and they might eat sweet corn, but if it's chickens that are getting killed, it's a coon or possum or maybe even a fox."

"I know that," Mom being a farm mother said, "but don't we call our traps muskrat traps?" which I admitted we did, and felt like a schoolteacher with a much older pupil that knew as much as the teacher.

Anyway, having to take the traps over to help Poetry set them meant I would get to leave early, just as soon as supper would be over, taking with me my night clothes, toothbrush, toothpaste, slippers and other stuff a mother thinks a boy ought to take with him when he goes to spend only one night in a friend's tent.

"I might not need a toothbrush," I said to Mom. "I can't brush while I'm asleep."

"You're to have breakfast at their house in the morning," Mom explained.

I answered, "But I *can't* brush after every meal, you know."

That made her come back with "Breakfast isn't *every* meal, my dear son. *Take* your toothbrush!"

Deciding it would make Mom happier if I *did* take it, I took it.

I went to the tool shed to get the steel traps, and was putting them into the front basket of my bicycle when Mixy, who had been taking a cat nap on the sloping cellar door, came meowing up at what I was doing, as much as if to say, "Are you going anywhere where a nice, friendly cat can't go?"

"I am," I said down to her. "I'm going over to Poetry's place and sleep in a tent."

"Meow," she answered back up at me, her gray-green eyes smoky with laziness.

"Besides," I went on, while she followed me and the bicycle over to the ivy arbor at our side door, "you never sleep at night anyway. You go gallivanting all

91

over everywhere looking for mice and rats. You're to stay home tonight and look after my folks."

Mom came out of the house with her overnight case, went to the tool shed and came out with another animal trap, our large, galvanized metal take-it-easy trap.

"Why the take-it-easy trap," I asked Mom, "when they asked for the other kind?"

"Because," Mom answered, "you can take it easy. Catch it alive, and the animal doesn't have to suffer for hours or even all night with its foot caught in a cruel-jawed trap, that's why."

I looked at Mom's tender brown eyes and remembered that they always got a hurt expression in them whenever she had to see anything suffer or when she even read about anybody or anything suffering, so I took a quick glance at the trap she was tying on top of her overnight case on top of my front basket, and said, "Sure, Mom, I'll take it and make them use it, if I can."

Charlotte Ann, Mom and Mixy followed me all the way to the walnut tree, the gate, and "Theodore Collins" on our mailbox. There they told me good-bye as well as a few other things Mom thought of at the last minute. Then my mother scooped Charlotte Ann up in her arms, set her in the swing and started her on a fast, back-and-forth swing until I could get gone.

"Beat it!" I said down to Mixy. "Scat, cat! I told you, you can't go!"

But that dopey-minded feline wouldn't beat it. Instead, she kept on brushing herself against my shins and between the wheels of my bike, and would get herself run over if I didn't get started while she was turning around to brush her way back through again.

I called out to Mom at the swing, "Will you please come to save this stubborn old cat from getting all nine of her lives killed right now, and all at once?"

As soon as I had a chance to get gone with the wind, away I went, racing toward a brand-new kind of adventure, sure I'd have a lot of fun before morning. And, who knows, I might hear Alexander the Coppersmith for sure—might even get to see with my own eyes one of Dragonfly's mother's flying saucers.

Chapter 9

SPENDING THE NIGHT in a tent with your almost best friend is one of the finest experiences ever a boy can have. Poetry and I had done it so many times the past few years, we knew almost exactly what it would be like.

Our clothes were hanging on a homemade costumer at the foot of the two cots, and all the light we needed was the moonlight filtering in through the plastic-netted tent window at the other end near our heads. Everything in the tent except our voices was very quiet, but outside were all the farm noises, such as once in a while a screech owl letting out his ghostly cry, a mother hog in a hollow sycamore tree making a mother-hog noise while her seven off-white little pigs made pigs of themselves, crickets chirping all around everywhere and— like it is on any hot late summer night—hundreds of cicadas rolling their drums with a noise that was like an orchestra with a hundred drumming musicians.

For a few jiffies while I was lying there in my hot cot just across from Poetry in his hot cot, listening to the night sounds, I let my mind's eye imagine what a harvest fly looked like—a cicada having quite a few different names, such as harvest fly and locust, an insect with a broad head, protruding eyes and transparent wings that fold over its body like a glass roof on a greenhouse.

My mind kept trying to drift off into a sea of dew, it being easy to go to sleep when locusts are drumming and ground crickets are plick-plocking a sing-song song. Also it seemed like there were several hundred small frogs having a family reunion in the swamp beyond the sycamore tree which is at the mouth of the cave.

I was also sort of listening in the direction of the Thompsons' chicken house to hear if any of Mrs. Thompson's laying hens were being stolen by a varmint of some kind.

"Do you know what?" Poetry whispered to me from three feet away.

"What?" I mumbled back.

"Baiting our trap with sardines like we did, we might catch a coon. A coon is like a house cat. It likes any kind of fish, as well as chickens and sweet corn and almost everything else."

"I hope we take it in the take-it-easy trap," I said, knowing that if we caught any varmint in one of the steel traps, as soon as Mom found out about it, she'd ask all kinds of questions, such as whether it had to suffer all night or whether it was a mother coon that had a family of babies somewhere that would have to be orphans.

Pretty soon, all the friendly sounds a boy hears at

night began to fade out as my mind started off into a sea of dew with Wynken, Blynken and Nod.

How long I slept I don't know, but I was startled out of my unconscious world by somebody's hands shaking me by the shoulders. I forced my eyes open, looked up to see something about the size of the mother bear in the story of Goldilocks and the three bears, leaning over my cot. "Hey, Bill!" a voice hissed. "Wake up! We've caught something big! Listen!"

I didn't have to listen, now that I was awake. From the direction of Poetry's chicken house there was a thumping and rattling and yowling such as I'd never heard in my life.

"We've caught the howling dog!" Poetry's excited voice exclaimed. "Come on, let's get up and go see."

We didn't bother to dress—only to slip into our slippers, and with Poetry carrying his flash camera and I my flashlight, we unzipped the door of the tent and out we went, hurrying toward whatever we were hurrying toward.

Such a sound!

"Might be a wildcat," I panted.

"Or a hundred of them," Poetry puffed back. Not only was there a yowling and bang-banging, but a whole henhouse full of scared hens and excited roosters were putting up such a clatter that we ran still faster to see what was the matter, dodging rosebushes and other shrubbery in the yard on our way toward whatever we had caught—either in one of the muskrat traps or in Mom's take-it-easy trap.

It took us only a few nerve-tingling minutes before we came to the corner of the chicken house, where the seventy-seven hens and maybe eight old roosters were still whooping it up like that many school kids let out for recess.

For some reason, we slowed down as we realized we might be in some kind of danger. I took a quick look around, saw an ax with its blade buried maybe an inch deep in a chopping block. When I eased the blade out by pumping the ax handle, I noticed a lot of feathers and blood on the block and around it, which maybe meant that Poetry's father had killed a young rooster there so they could have fried chicken for dinner. Or else, maybe it meant that the wild animal we had in our trap had already killed and eaten at least one chicken this very night.

And then, what to my wondering eyes should appear in the circle of my flashlight's light, but something black and white and furry.

"It's a skunk!" Poetry exclaimed. "We've caught a skunk!" With that disgusted remark, he lifted his camera, focused it and let go with a picture.

"Skunk, nothing," I disagreed. "If it was a skunk, it'd smell all over the place!"

As quick as Poetry's flash camera's flash, there was the beginning of silence, except for one still-scared old hen that kept on cackling, like a woman on a Sugar Creek party line who didn't know all the other women had hung up and was going on to finish a story she had started.

97

One thing for sure, whatever we'd caught wasn't in either of the steel traps, but was inside the wire network of the take-it-easy trap. In the three-foot circle of my flash, two fiery eyes were staring back at me, and the black and white whatever-it-was crouched like it was ready to spring.

Then Poetry came to with a snicker and a guffaw as he exclaimed, "Well, well, well! Now we know the black-and-white truth. Our chicken thief is somebody's dumb old house cat!"

Hearing my almost best friend say what he said in such a sarcastic way, fired my temper a little, because "somebody's dumb old house cat" was a very special friend of mine. I knew the minute we were within seven feet of the take-it-easy trap that the wildcat we had caught was Mixy herself.

"Of all the dumb things for a cat to do!" I scolded her, as I stooped to open the trap and let her out.

But say! Do you know what? All of a hissing sudden she began to spit at me, to jump and struggle against the bars of her jail like it was my fault she had gotten caught and I was an enemy of some kind.

While we were getting our black and white wildcat out, there was a movement behind us like a lady's skirt across the grass, and it was Poetry's mother in a long, green housecoat coming to see what all the fuss was about. When she saw Mixy, she couldn't believe her eyes. But as soon as she realized we'd caught the chicken thief, if we had, she said, "I'm going to phone your mother right now and tell her. I promised her

I would call just as soon as we caught anything, and in what trap."

"Mixy isn't anything," I objected, "except a dumb old house cat that doesn't know enough not to go snooping around a wild animal trap. It might be better to wait till morning anyway 'cause Mom's been having insomnia the last few nights, and she won't sleep a wink if the phone rings in the middle of the night."

"Besides," Poetry chimed in, "you know what happens when a party line phone rings at night. Every mother on the line will wake up and get up and stagger to the phone to eavesdrop, and it wouldn't be fair to an innocent cat to get gossiped about at midnight, even if the innocent cat is a dumb bunny."

Poetry's mother's *mother* spirit came to life then, and she began to pet Mixy, who for some reason had become as quiet as a worried mouse, and was actually purring in my arms.

"Poor little darling!" Poetry's mother cooed to our big fat cat. "You're hungry! I'll take you into the house and get you some milk."

"Hungry!" Poetry disagreed. "That cat's already eaten half a can of sardines!"

I looked at the floor of the trap Mixy'd just been caught in, and it was as bare as Old Mother Hubbard's cupboard.

Well, it seemed we ought to bait the trap again to try to catch the real chicken thief, which we all knew Mixy wasn't, but had only been wandering around in the neighborhood like house cats do at night and, smelling the sardines, had walked innocently into our trap.

I hoped it would be a lesson to her not to follow a Collins boy around.

Not having any more sardines, we baited the take-it-easy trap with a small piece of fresh meat from the Thompsons' refrigerator. Then taking a look at the two steel traps under the chicken house window to see if we had caught even a rat in them and hadn't, I gave Mixy strict orders to go home and take a long cat nap like she always does after every meal, like I have to brush my teeth after every meal.

Poetry's mother all of a sudden made Poetry and me come into the kitchen to eat a piece apiece of blueberry pie. She offered Mixy a little milk in a saucer on the floor, but Mixy wasn't interested. Instead, she went snooping in the direction of the wastebasket in the corner.

"She smells the empty sardine can," Poetry's mother explained. "That cat's starved for fish. You boys'll have to go fishing and catch her a sunfish or something tomorrow." That didn't sound exactly like something a boy's mother would say.

Well, there was quite a lot of night left to sleep away, so it seemed a good idea for us to go back to bed. What to do with a fish-hungry cat was the problem, because the two steel traps under the chicken house window were still baited with sardines, so Poetry's mother decided she'd lock Mixy up in their screened porch.

Back in the tent, Poetry and I climbed into our still-hot cots and started to try to go to sleep when it seemed like I heard a strange sound outside somewhere.

I was quick out of my cot and looking out the nylon-netted opening at the front of the tent—and that's when we *did* hear for sure a sound of something or somebody from the direction of the henhouse, the weirdest, middle-of-the-night outdoor sound I'd ever heard. It was a little like a screech owl—or maybe a blue jay or a red-headed woodpecker with a bad cold, which was scared and had a trembling voice.

Out of our cots we went again, slippers on, pajamas flapping in the breeze we were making as we ran, my flashlight making a long white cone-shaped hole in the darkness, Poetry carrying his flash camera, ready to snap a shot of anything we had caught. It took only a few minutes of dodging shrubbery in their yard before we came to the hedge that separates the lawn from their orchard and, squeezing through a narrow place, came to where the traps were. But they were as bare as Old Mother Hubbard's cupboard—not bare of food, but of any kind of varmint. *We hadn't caught anything!*

Swinging my flash around, not a creature was stirring, not even a mouse.

Poetry let out a hissing sigh, saying, "What's going

on in our minds, anyway? Are we just hearing things, or what?"

On the way back to the tent, we had just reached the opening in the hedge when Poetry stopped ahead of me and exclaimed, "There it is again! Down by the mouth of the cave!"

And he was right. Now that the sound didn't have to come through the walls of a tent, it was as clear as a school bell on a cold frosty morning, and the sound was like that of a howling dog—a long-toned, high-pitched wailing squall.

I stayed stock-still, glued by my fear of what I might be hearing. I was also beginning to tremble. It was different from hearing a howling dog in the daytime. This was at *night!* And it wasn't Dragonfly hearing it, or his superstitious mother. It was I, Bill Collins, Theodore Collins' first and worst son, who was hearing it—or *was* I me? Maybe I wasn't myself at all, but somebody else; or maybe I was back there in my hot cot in the tent asleep and this was only my subconscious mind sailing off in a sea of dew.

"There he is again!" Poetry cried. "He's got one of our old hens down by the cave or in a den in the sycamore tree!"

It was the same kind of sound a grown-up chicken makes when a boy catches her in his mother's garden and is carrying her to the fence to throw her back over into the chicken yard—also like the sound a young rooster makes when your father is getting ready to put his head on the chopping block to have him for dinner, like it is scared even worse than half to death.

"Let's go see if we can save her!" Poetry ahead of me called back over his shoulder, already on a puffing run toward the cave.

And away we both went, past Old Whitey's tree house and down the sloping barnyard in the direction of where it sounded like the old hen's dying squawk had sounded like it had come from.

Poetry, beside or behind or ahead of me, cried out, "Did you see that?"

I had already seen it—or that, or whatever it was— a light above the swamp, going on and off in the trees somewhere. "It's still on!" I said. "See it?" I, myself, with my own two wide-awake eyes was seeing it, a bright light as powerful as a three-batteried flash- light was actually shining through the heavily leafed trees about as far out in the swamp as the muskrat pond.

"It's moving!" Poetry cried, his voice trembling. "It's taking off across the sky!"

"It's a flying saucer!" Our two voices squawked at the same time. "Dragonfly's mother was right!"

We were both stopped stock-still now, our fear like contact glue, holding our feet fast to the ground.

Not only had there been a light flashing on and off, and not only had there been a light as big as a load of alfalfa hay moving out across the trees in the swamp, but there had also been a whirring noise, like a motor running, kind of like a squeaking wheel, a dying hen and a howling dog. *We* had seen it! *We* had heard it! And *we* were two honest-to-goodness earth people who had seen a space vehicle of some kind right in Sugar Creek territory!

And now what to do!

"I've got it!" Poetry beside me exclaimed. "Let's go up to Old Man Paddler's place where the girl and her father are camped and tell them, and they'll put the news in the *Indianapolis News,* and our pictures, and everything! When they ask us if we heard a sound, or what the sound sounded like, we'll tell them it sounded like the squawking of a dying hen."

We started as fast as we could in the direction of the shortcut that led to Old Man Paddler's place, when we were startled by another sound behind us—running footsteps. I quick whirled around, shined my flashlight in several directions and saw coming toward us, making a beeline for the cave, a furry, fiery-eyed animal of some kind. It had a broad head and pointed nose; and as the gray thing swished past the sycamore tree, I saw that its ten-or-more-inches-long tail had black rings around it. He was running pell-mell toward the big ash tree that grew not more than forty feet from the sycamore. Up that tree, like a scared cat with a neighborhood dog after it, that wild animal went.

"It's a coon!" Poetry cried. "And there's a hound after it."

And there was. A big black and tan coonhound swept into the circle of my flashlight not more than

104

fifty feet behind the coon, getting to the tree just as Ringtail reached the first branch about twenty feet from the ground. Then it seemed the whole neighborhood came to life with a wild bawling and barking and howling, as that hound let loose with a happy, excited and also worried voice, as if to say to whoever he belonged to, "Come and get it! I've chased him up a tree for you!"

"It's Silent Sal!" Poetry cried.

And it was. Circus' father's silent trailer, which never let loose with a bark or howl or even a whimper when she was trailing the scent of a varmint, until she caught a possum or coon or chased one up a tree. Then it would be like somebody had pulled out all the stops of a giant-sized pipe organ and turned a pack of hounds loose to chase up and down the keyboard.

If we needed any more proof that it was Silent Sal, Circus' father's long-nosed, long-voiced black and tan hound, we right away had it, 'cause running through the woods making a clomp-clomp-clomping sound were the footsteps of several human beings—Circus, Big Jim and Dragonfly, pell-melling themselves toward the ash tree where Silent Sal was still whooping it up like a pack of Indians on the warpath.

Chapter 10

THE MINUTE those three other members of our gang reached the ash tree, Big Jim, who was carrying a powerful electric lantern, turned it on, sending a long white cone of light up into the trees all around, searching for whatever Silent Sal's baying voice was telling us was up there somewhere. In only a few fast seconds the light came to focus on a gray, shining-eyed animal swaying in the branches of the ash tree.

"*That,*" my disappointed mind told me, "is your flying saucer—Big Jim's powerful electric lantern!" *That* was what we had seen moving above the musk-rat pond, lighting up the treetops, then going off, and also on again.

What a disappointment!

There wasn't any flying saucer or flying cigar or boxcar!

But my mind wasn't going to give up easily. So I came out with "But if there *isn't* any saucer or anything, what was that squawking noise we heard up there in the trees?"

It took us only a few minutes of excited talking and explaining to find out what was what and why, and how come Circus, Big Jim and Dragonfly were there with Silent Sal.

"Some varmint had been getting into our chickens almost every night," Circus explained—or began to explain—when Big Jim cut in with "Ours too almost every night, so we decided that whatever it was, if it came snooping around tonight we'd put Silent Sal on its trail."

Big Jim and Circus had decided it together—they being the biggest members of our gang and not wanting to tell the rest of us their plans or we'd all have wanted to go too. "We had enough trouble getting our parents to let *us* do it," Big Jim explained. "If we'd asked you guys to come along, we'd have had eight more parents to worry about, with all twelve of them worrying about us."

"How come you brought Dragonfly along then?" Poetry's squawky voice asked.

"Dad and Mother don't know it," our sneezy little friend explained. "They painted my room yesterday, and I had to sleep in the motel. I picked the unit at the end, closest to the woods." If you've read *The Old Stranger's Secret at Sugar Creek* you know that the Gilberts own and run the Tall Corn Motel.

I looked at Dragonfly's pinched little face with its crooked nose that turns south at the end, and decided to ask, "What if your mother gets insomnia tonight and gets up and goes out to see if you're asleep and all right, and finds you gone?"

That question scared him a little it seemed, 'cause

107

he all of a sudden said, "You shouldn't have thought of that. Maybe she's already awake, with all the noise Silent Sal is making."

Dragonfly almost yelled what he was saying because Silent Sal was still sounding like the Sugar Creek High School orchestra when it plays on a cold day at a football game.

"Might as well all go home," Big Jim decided. "Old Ringtail's scared enough now to stay out of anybody's chicken house tonight. Let's get Dragonfly back into his motel room before his folks come looking for him."

"What about tomorrow night?" Poetry asked. "That coon'll forget all about what happened tonight and'll be right back stealing and killing chickens. I'm for shooting her and throwing her into the muskrat pond. The turtles can have her for breakfast. Here, give me the rifle." He reached for the .22 Big Jim was holding, the rifle being pointed away from all of us all the time. It's a rule of safety never to let a loaded gun be pointed at or toward anything you don't want to shoot. If a gun goes off accidentally, somebody or something might get killed.

Big Jim stepped back. "Didn't you notice how large she was? Look at her. She might be a mother coon expecting a family of babies!"

I took a look at Poetry's fat face to see how he would take an answer like that, he being still pretty angry at having two of his mother's best laying hens killed the night before.

"Besides," said Big Jim, who seemed to be on the coon's side, "coons travel in families, hardly ever alone. Old Silent might have trailed only *one* of them, and if we shoot this one we might kill the one that's not guilty."

Forgetting for a few seconds that Little Jim wasn't with us, it seemed I was expecting his tender heart to make him speak up and say, like he does whenever any chicken-killing varmint has to get killed in the neighborhood, "She wasn't *trying* to be *mean!* She was just *hungry!*"

Big Jim shoved another long bright beam of light up into the branches of the ash, searched around until its circle focused on the big fat coon, this time lighting up only the black-ringed tail, the rest of the chicken thief, if it *was* a chicken thief, hidden behind the large branch she was on.

Silent Sal, even though being held tightly by her collar by Circus' strong hands, was finding it as hard to be quiet as a boy does when he has to stay in the house on a rainy day.

"Let's go," Big Jim ordered us. "She has a right to live until she's been proved guilty. If we'd caught her in the *act* of stealing, it might be different. But it *is* out of season to hunt coon and we could get into trouble for hunting and killing one out of season," which, up to now, not a one of us had thought of to say.

In all the excitement, I'd forgotten for a minute the sound of a dying old hen we'd heard maybe thir-

109

teen minutes ago. But a boy can't forget about hearing a sound like that—not for very long, especially when all of a rasping sudden it comes again, this time from the woods in the direction of Old Man Paddler's cabin—a harsh, grating, long-toned squawk that sent the shivers all over me.

"A mountain lion maybe," Circus suggested. "What do you say, Silent Sal?"

Say, that hound's black back was already bristling like a dog's back does when it is getting acquainted with a strange dog it's not sure is going to be friendly.

Hearing that ghostly cry, Poetry said, "Whatever it is, it's after our chickens again!"

"Ours, you mean," Circus disagreed. "It came from the direction of *our* house."

"It could be *ours*," Big Jim put in. "Let's go find out whose!" And away we went, not sure of our directions but trying to go toward the sound.

Circus was holding tight to the other end of the leash he had snapped on Silent Sal's collar so she wouldn't take off on the trail of the first varmint scent her snuffling nose came across, and we might not know where she was until she treed something.

As we rambled along, the sound of the dying chicken kept repeating itself every few seconds, which made it easy to keep on going in the right direction.

We'd been huffing and puffing along for maybe nine minutes when Circus pulled up short, stopping Silent Sal, and saying, "Wait, everybody!"

We stopped and waited, and here is what he said:

"How come that old hen doesn't stop squawking? You'd think she'd be dead by now! That's the tenth time she's done it—starting like she was being killed by something or other, then stopping and starting again, the same way!"

"Yeah," I agreed. "First, she gets killed by something, then she comes to life again, and keeps on dying and coming to life. Hens can't do that!"

Dragonfly didn't help any when he came out with "A *ghost* hen could."

We were within maybe fifty yards of the squawking now. At Big Jim's shushing orders, we all stopped talking and walking and stayed stopped in our tracks, keeping ourselves in the shadow of the spreading maple tree we were under, the moonlight dappling our faces and clothes as it filtered through the branches.

"Sounds like maybe she's caught in a trap or something, maybe in the wire fence between the swamp and Old Man Paddler's woods," I suggested.

Big Jim came back with "But how did somebody's old hen get this far from home, all by herself?"

Dragonfly's answer didn't make any more sense than a lot of his other ideas do, but believing what he did, it must have made sense to him: "She could have fallen out of the flying saucer that's been skimming around the sky every night—and maybe she landed in the thorn tree beside the stile."

While we were standing there in a half-crouch like we were afraid something or somebody would see us,

111

Poetry came up with what seemed like a good idea: "Let's keep our flashlights off, so if there's a little green man from Mars or from some other planet, I can get a color picture of him. Our lights might scare him and he'd go flying back to wherever he came from."

Again we started toward where we thought we should go, creeping cautiously along from the shadow of one tree to another till we came to within what was maybe sixty feet from where the start-and-stop dying hen was. We were crouched now under the umbrellalike branches of a papaw tree, one of its foot-long leaves drooping in front of my eyes, making it hard to see what I couldn't see anyway.

Beside me, I could hear Dragonfly trying to stop a sneeze as he whispered to me, "I'm allergic to chicken feathers."

"You're too far away for that," Circus who'd heard him disagreed. "That's the overripe smell of these papaws," which it maybe was, papaws getting ripe this time of year, looking like short, very fat bananas, the extra-ripe ones being like custard on the inside, having a sickening taste; and I might even be allergic to one myself, because just looking at one a barefoot boy has stepped on, and smelling it at the same time, always gives me a headache.

It was too dark to see if any of us had stepped on a ripe papaw, but somebody must have because I began to be sick at my stomach, very, *very* sick. Like a cowboy on a bucking bronco exploding out of a chute at a rodeo, I went storming out of our hiding place under the tree into the moonlight on the opposite side of the tree and for a few minutes sounded like a dying hen myself, or maybe like a young Rhode Island Red rooster learning to crow.

As soon as I had finished swallowing backward, I felt better and was able to come back into our nervous little circle where Silent Sal wasn't so silent but had a muffled growling in her throat, like any minute she would make a dive toward something she was seeing, and start barking.

"You know what it sounds like?" Big Jim now asked, and didn't wait for anybody to answer. "She's *not* caught in the fence. She's *up* somewhere. Up in a tree, maybe."

One thing for sure, my ears now told me, the squawking *was* coming from some direction of up.

"Listen, you guys," Poetry said. "If I'm going to get a picture of whatever it is, I'd better do it before it flies away."

That seemed like the best thing to do right now—if anything was—so, with Poetry leading the way, his camera poised, we began inching ourselves along after him like five snails in a race with each other to see who could crawl the slowest, following the shadow of the shrubbery that bordered the fence, Circus being especially careful not to let Silent Sal make a howling dog of herself. If that old black and tan hound should let loose one of her own wailing squalls, whatever was up a tree or telephone pole or hanging suspended from a flying saucer, would go zooming off into the sky and we'd never get a picture of it—*or her, or him, or them.*

Any minute now we'd be near enough, Poetry would focus his camera, press the button, there'd be a blinding flash of light, and we'd have our proof that there really was a flying saucer or something, *if* there was.

"Sh-h!"

It was Big Jim shushing us—not a one of us needing to be shushed. There was a kind of scary sound now, coming from the left like some animal creeping along—*not toward the fence, but toward us!* There was a now-and-then snapping of a twig being stepped on or a pile of leaves being stumbled into, then there would be silence for maybe ten or more nervous seconds. There wasn't a thing we could see, yet we kept on hearing those footsteps. Whatever was coming, was keeping in the shadows like we were.

Cold and hot and nervous chills began racing up and down my spine, for right then I was not only hearing a cautious movement but was also seeing something as large as the middle-sized bear in the story of Goldilocks and the three bears. Whatever it was, it was trying not to be seen.

Now it was standing on two legs, sort of stooped over. No, it was *down* on four legs, crouching and crawling at the same time. To get from one shadowed place to another, it had to move across a few feet of

114

moonlit space, and that's when I caught a glimpse of something bright reflected in the moonlight.

It seemed like time was standing as still as we were —all of us, except Poetry who was ahead of us, like a middle-sized bear himself. The very second he would snap his picture, we would all turn on our different flashlights, and get to see what was what and why.

And then, all of a blinding sudden, the whole place exploded into action. There was a quick movement ahead of us, a shadow of something as big as a small gorilla leaped out from behind the black bole of a tree, a powerful light swooshed on, lighting up the shrubbery we were hiding behind, our faces and all of us, and Poetry himself on his hands and knees about ten feet ahead of us.

A split second later, after the on-and-off flash, another light came on. In fact, four blinding lights, like a monster with *four* five-inch-wide eyes all in a row, were focused on us.

Dragonfly let out a scream: "It's little green men from Mars. They're trying to blind us!" He stumbled back, bumped into me, lost his balance and fell, while the rest of us held our hands before our faces to keep from being blinded.

At the same time, the dying hen stopped squawking and there came megaphoning through the woods and along the bayou and the swamp the long-toned, howling squall of a lonely hound.

Pandemonium broke out then, as Silent Sal fought

herself loose from Circus, lit out in the direction of the fence and, in a series of wild bawlings and howls and also short sharp barks, began leaping wildly around the base of an elm tree that grew there only a few feet from the stile.

Chapter 11

WHAT CAN YOU do at a time of night like that, when there isn't a thing in the world or out of it you can thing of *to* do, and you can't think anyway?

The four bright lights were still on us. Dragonfly was still on the ground, shielding his eyes with his arm. And the sounds of the howling dog and the squawking hen were still coming from somewhere up in the elm tree, around the base of which Silent Sal was a noisy gal, leaping up and squalling, "Treed!"

As abruptly now as the four eyes had been turned on us, they went off, and I heard a worried voice calling: "What is it, Romaine? Are you all right?"

My blurred vision showed me, coming across a stretch of moonlit grass between the hedgerow and the beginning of Old Man Paddler's place, a tallish man limping along. With him, on the end of a leash, was a nervous, excited dog, straining and pulling and almost dragging the man after him.

Dragonfly, seeing what I was seeing, let out an explosive *"It's Alexander! He's alive!"*

The tall, bareheaded man was wearing a red plaid robe; and one leg from the knee down to the ankle,

I noticed, was snow-white and almost twice as big around as a man's ordinary leg ought to be.

Poetry seemed to have his mind on something else. He had shoved the long powerful beam of his flashlight up into the elm tree where we'd been hearing the sound of the squawking chicken. A jiffy later he exploded with: "Look at your dying old hen, will you! It's *not* an old hen! It's a loudspeaker!"

I did look, and saw a bell-shaped something-or-other, the size and shape of an old-fashioned phonograph player's speaker. Silent Sal was silent now, sniffing lazily around the base of the tree. Then she came kind of sheepishly back to Circus and to our little circle of excitement, her sad, wrinkled face drooping like she was ashamed for barking up a tree when the tree was as bare of any varmint as Mother Hubbard's cupboard had been when she had gone to it "to get her poor dog a bone."

The nervous, excited, copper-colored dog was still straining at his leash trying to get Silent Sal interested in acting like a dog ought to act when it meets a dog stranger. But Sal, now that she had been fooled by something that was nothing, yawned, stretched and lay down at Circus' feet looking up at him with sad eyes as if to say, "I refuse to be fooled again. That red-haired, copper-colored dog is *not* a dog. I've just been dreaming."

And it seemed like maybe she had been, and maybe we all were, 'cause if there was ever in the world a dog that looked and acted like Alexander the Coppersmith, it was the mongrel in our circle, wiggling all over the place, sniffling at everything and everybody.

There'd been a little excited talk between the man and the girl he had called Romaine, and some of it was beginning to make a few things clear to me, and to help put the pieces of a crazy mixed-up picture puzzle into place.

Answering the tall man's question, "What is it, Romaine? Are you all right?" the girl had called back to him with a worried tone of voice: "Father! You shouldn't be up! Of course, I'm all right! Only I've taken a movie of something I wasn't looking for—the nice boys I saw in the swamp yesterdey. Remember? One of them killed the water moccasin for me."

I wasn't sure right then that I was a "nice" boy, 'cause I was disgruntled in my mind at having my ideas about a flying saucer exploded. One question was whirling around in my thoughts: Was the copper-colored dog wiggling all around us a real dog, or was I still back under the spreading branches of the beech-nut tree beside the black widow stump, sound asleep with an unsound mind?

Right then, something else began to happen. There was the sound of a motor, and from the direction of Old Man Paddler's cabin came the headlamps of a car, bouncing along in the lane that was used by forest rangers when they patrolled the woods. A red light was flashing on and off on top of the car, and a powerful spotlight searched the area all around until it came to focus on us, the car itself coming to a stop about fifty feet from where we were, and a voice calling through a loud speaker: "This is the police! Have you seen anything of a lost boy?"

But there was another voice coming from the police car—a woman's voice, calling "Roy Gilbert! What on earth are you doing out here in this ghostly woods?" And it was Dragonfly's mother.

It was Dragonfly's father too, we found out in a few minutes more, when a tallish, gray-brown-haired man wearing a green shirt and gray flannel trousers came hurrying with Mrs. Gilbert right out into the middle of all our other excitement.

I didn't exactly like to see what I had to see right then, which was Dragonfly's worrisome mother make a running dive for her son, throw her arms around him, and cry and say, "What on earth made you leave your room? You've had us worried half to death!"

I felt sorry for Dragonfly having to have his mother cry all over him with everybody looking on, like he was just a little kid and not a good-sized boy able to take care of himself.

Next day, back at our place, when I was telling my parents about our exciting night and how embarrassing it must have been to Dragonfly, Dad disagreed with me, saying, "A son hasn't any business causing his parents a lot of needless worry. He shouldn't have climbed out that motel window and gone chasing off with Circus and Big Jim like that."

I was still on Dragonfly's side, so I answered Dad, saying, "But he almost had to—believing what he did.

If he'd asked his parents first, they wouldn't have let him go—and just think what he'd have missed out on!"

Mom put in her own idea then, saying, "I can understand the boy, having a normal son of my own, but let's not blame his parents for worrying, especially his mother. She almost *had* to cry over finding him, believing what *she* did, that her son was maybe kidnapped. A son is worth more than a million dollars to a parent."

I took a quick look at my parents and it seemed like maybe they were trying to tell me something. Maybe they liked their own first and worst son more than anything in the world, unless maybe it was their first and worst daughter, who right that minute was out by the tool shed, over halfway up Dad's ladder which he had left standing there after having been up on the roof trying to fix a small leak.

My mother made a fast swooshing dash for the ladder and got there just in time to catch her daughter who was almost all the way to the top. The ladder was losing its balance, and in another jiffy somebody would have fallen down and cracked her crown.

When Mom turned back to us, carrying her unhappy daughter, she looked several sharp arrows at Dad and said, "Somebody's first and worst *husband* is not supposed to leave a ladder standing!"

That sent my mind back to last night, to the elm tree beside the stile, the loudspeaker hidden in the branches of the tree, and, at the base of the tree, Old

Man Paddler's long aluminum ladder. "That's what happened to the girl's father," I told my folks—having learned it last night. "Last week he set the ladder up against the tree and climbed up to attach a loud-speaker up there. He did get it tied and was on his way down when the ladder slipped and he fell and broke his leg, which is how come he was wearing a walking cast."

I explained several other things to my folks, while Charlotte Ann whimpered and squirmed, wanting to go back to the ladder and climb up all the way to the top to prove she was a big girl and could take care of herself. Dad went *to* the ladder and, with a sort of set face, hung it where it belonged when not in use, on ladder hooks on the garage wall.

There was an expression on Dad's face that seemed to say he was a grown-up person himself and didn't exactly enjoy having somebody's first and worst wife telling him what to do and why—and also *when*. As soon as he had the ladder in place and Charlotte Ann was pumping water into her drinking cup and throwing it over the iron kettle into the butterflies' drinking puddle, he came back to Mom and me. Bowing low like an old-fashioned knight in a schoolbook, he took Mom's hand, kissed it on the back, and said, "At your service always, Madam!"

* * *

The next week was maybe one of the most impor-tant of our lives. The gang not only got the mystery of the howling dog cleared up, but the man who, we found out, was a lecturer on wildlife, actually hired us to help him and his daughter Romaine get a lot of moving and still pictures of animal life in our territory. We also helped him get tape recordings of as many wildlife voices as we could—crickets plick-plocking, tree frogs trilling and bullfrogs thundering. There were enough flash camera shots at night to make any boy's superstitious mother think she was seeing flying saucers above the swamp.

Their copper-colored dog which, we found out, was named Napoleon Bonaparte, was so much like Alexander the Coppersmith that he really could have *been* him if we all hadn't known he wasn't.

Near the end of the week, after we'd helped the man get about all the pictures and sounds of wildlife he wanted in our territory, and he and Romaine were getting ready to break camp and move to Northern Indiana to get other pictures and sounds in the sand dunes there, it seemed like one of the most interesting chapters in our lives was about to end. Getting pictures at night had been the *most* interesting when we helped the professor set up his "camera trap" as he called it. First we would hide his loudspeaker in a tree or along the creek or near a beaver dam. Then, when he was ready, he'd turn on his tape recorder, and all kinds of distress calls would go echoing through the woods and along the bayou; and almost every time, if we waited long enough, some animal would get caught in the act of being himself.

It was after the professor had broken his leg and

had had to stay around camp that he and his daughter Romaine had hit upon the plan to use a recording of Napoleon's howls as a signal for her to hurry back to camp, as her father needed her for something, and she would use her whistle to answer him.

And now, tomorrow was their last day, and we were feeling pretty sad. We were lying in the grass near the Black Widow Stump, talking and trying to make up our minds whether to go in swimming or just laze around awhile first, then mozey on up to the professor's camp, when the professor himself came limping along in the path that borders the bayou. Running ahead of him in all directions was his dog that looked and acted like Alexander the Coppersmith. The man was carrying binoculars on a leather strap around his neck, and every now and then he would stop and write something in a notebook. Then he would use his binoculars to scan the sky and the trees all around. Then he would write again. Just that minute Napoleon Bonaparte scared up a cottontail that went scooting toward a brushpile not far from the leaning linden tree, and the professor quick whipped up his camera and took a moving picture of it.

It was while his camera was sweeping the area all around that it picked up six boys lying in the shade of the beechnut tree, and he came over to have a little visit with us.

After talking awhile and telling us he had arranged to give one of his fall lectures at Sugar Creek, he said, "Romaine and I have a problem. The first of September, we're moving into a home in a new housing project in Indianapolis. When we signed the lease we had to agree to a no-pet clause. That means Romaine will have to surrender Napoleon. We can't bear the thought of having him put to sleep, so—well, we wonder if any of you boys would like to own a very loyal dog. He is a little nervous, perhaps; but even though he is a mongrel, he would make some boy very happy."

Circus was the first to answer, saying, "He and Silent Sal seem to get along pretty well together, but we already have three other dogs—"

Big Jim straightened up from having been studying a hole in the ground near the Black Widow Stump where Napoleon had been digging, and said, "He doesn't have any pedigree, I suppose."

"No one knows his ancestry," the professor answered. "Romaine found him about a year ago when we were visiting the humane society. There was a litter of copper-colored puppies someone had brought in, two of which were exactly alike, except that one had a white mark on his throat. That was the one Romaine wanted. Next day she decided she wanted the other one so she would have a pair, but we were too late. Right after we had left, a red-haired boy had come with his parents and adopted him."

Boy, oh boy! Did *that* set my mind in a happy whirl! Before any of the rest of the gang could say anything, I quick spoke up, saying, "I know a boy who would like to have a dog like that." And then with all of us helping a little, we told the professor the story of Alexander the Coppersmith, the battle with the wildcat, and everything.

When I got home that afternoon, my father put in a long-distance call to Memory City to a family named Sensenbrother. That is why my red aunt, her husband and a boy named Wally Sensenbrother came driving as fast as they could to Sugar Creek to see if Wally would like to adopt Napoleon Bonaparte to take the place of Alexander the Coppersmith.

"Do you know what?" I asked Dad while he and I were down in the barn doing the chores to get them over with early.

Dad, who was up in the haymow throwing down alfalfa for the cows, called down the ladder to ask, "No, what?"

I had just found three hen's eggs in a new nest on the middle shelf of Dad's tool cabinet and was feeling proud of myself for finding them. I answered him with a very happy voice, saying up to him, "I've just thought up a new name for Wally to call Napoleon. He could name him—"

A pile of hay the size of three chicken coops came landing with a swoosh at my feet as I finished what I had started to say: "A good name for him would be 'Happiness!' "

Down came another bunch of alfalfa, even bigger, along with Dad's question, "Why 'Happiness'?"

"Because," I yelled up to him, *happiness was born a twin!*"

While Dad and I were flying around, doing all the different things a boy and his father get to do together before supper, it seemed like I had never felt so happy in my life before, just imagining *how* happy Wally was going to be when he saw Alexander the Coppersmith's twin brother and found out that he could have him for his own special dog friend for as long as he lived.

I was so happy that when I got to the house a little later, I decided to try to make our old black and white cat happy too. First, I called to her to come and get her supper of fresh warm milk which I was ready to pour into her feeding pan near the grape arbor.

Three seconds after I had raised my voice she was there, mewing up at me, and acting like she had even more than nine lives, all of them starving to death. "Wait, cat," I said down to her, holding the milk pitcher high out of her reach. "I have something to show you first." I then quick took out of my shirt pocket a picture of a cat caught in a take-it-easy trap, which picture Poetry had had developed and given me when we were down in the woods that afternoon.

"Here, kitty, kitty, kitty, *nice* kitty, kitty, kitty. Here is something you ought to take a good look at." I handed the picture down to her so she could see herself as others had seen her at midnight quite a few weeks ago.

But do you know what? That black and white feline took one disgusted sniff at that snapshot, gave me a smoky-eyed stare, and started acting as though Poetry's snapshot showing what a dumb bunny cat she was, was the picture of somebody else's cat. As her rough tongue went lickety-slurp-slurp-slurp while she lapped up the milk I had just poured for her, it seemed like she was saying, "I know that picture *looks* like me, but it *wasn't* me. That was one of my cat sisters. Just in case you didn't know it, sir, *I was born a twin too.*"

Moody Press, a ministry of the Moody Bible Institute, is designed for education, evangelization and edification. If we may assist you in knowing more about Christ and the Christian life, please write us without obligation to:
Moody Press, c/o MLM, Chicago, Illinois 60610.